All Money Ain't Good Money

A Tale of Greed

Jameelah Kareem

ISBN   978-0-615-41182-8

Cover design by: elizedesigns.com
Photography by: iamjamesjohnson.com
www.TaleofGreed.com

Dedication

To all the young women who realize the worth of their life
is made up in more then just dollar bills.
Also to those who are struggling to find that worth;
it will reveal in time.

"If you don't think enough, someone will figure out how to do it for you."
- Chantel

1

~ Broken Families ~

Introducing Simone

Simone was born into a family of wealth, where education and a focused career choice was the root of all success. Work hard and even harder and you will have everything you desire. Anything you can materially think of is yours if you handle your business right was the way of her world. Her mother, Mrs. Hayes, was a well established high profile lawyer who stressed the importance of education to Simone. She knew she wanted her daughter to follow in her path and be financially set and successful. Her father, Mr. Hayes, was a music teacher at the local high school. He loved his job but always had a dream of opening his own business. He never took the time to start it because he knew he had to continue to work in order to help provide for his wife and daughter. Mrs. Hayes would not be pleased with a struggling, self employed entrepreneur. He also knew that he couldn't completely rely on Mrs. Hayes for the financial support. Even though she held a slight resentment against her husband for being the secondary provider, leaving her to be the primary, she loved him dearly.

Mr. Hayes was always more of a free spirit who focused more on family and emotions and the little things in life. He wasn't as worldly as his wife and always believed success came from a strong guidance from God. The main thing he tried to teach Simone was that good deeds return with even better rewards. On the other hand, his wife was materialistic in all senses of the word. She believed money was everything and without it her life would crumble. Simone was stuck in the middle of the two. She was Daddy's little girl but longed for her mother to care for her the same way her father did.

During Simone's childhood her mother was always so busy with work that she ignored her motherly duties and even sometimes she ignored her wifely duties. Her focus was always her career no matter what. Making money she thought was enough to raise and complete a family. Her husband got little attention and so did Simone. She knew after having Simone that she positively didn't want to have any more kids. Her mindset was too selfish to put her time and energy into another person again. She wasn't good with raising a child and it hurt Simone in ways that were indescribable. The lack of love and attention made Simone underestimate the power of real love in general. Only time would tell the scars that would leave.

Most of her younger days were spent playing alone in her freshly manicured backyard on her wooden swing set as her father watched on from inside. There was always the feeling of emptiness that lingered with Simone from the lack of attention she received from her mother. Being the only child didn't help either. The boredom and routine life of the upper middle class suburbs drove her closely to point of insanity. Seeking new and inventive ways to entertain herself she dreamt up imaginative and creative ways that she believed would be her ticket out of that town. Hopes of being a singer, model, actress and Hollywood A-lister filled her mind as she was consumed with the flashy lifestyle from whatever the media dished out on TV, magazines, billboards and the radio. By the time she was nearing the end of high school, her career goals and aspirations were the exact opposite of what her mother tried to instill in her. The original plan was to attend Princeton University but not long after acceptance her plan began to stray.

Introducing Chantel

Ms. Wilson gave birth to Chantel when she was only fourteen years old; about to turn fifteen. She absolutely wasn't ready for it but situations happen like that all the time around her neighborhood. Her environment was filled with teen pregnancies, drugs, and low income and non educated families. Ms. Wilson was well beyond her years of fourteen, not only her mind but her looks. She attracted not only young boys her age but also grown men. She was beautiful, with a caramel complexion and hazel eyes with long curled eye lashes. Her eyes were so devious, she could get anything she wanted just by the look in them. She had soft, shoulder length, honey blonde hair. She was hot around her way and everyone knew it, especially herself. She had guys sweating her all around the neighborhood. The way that Ms. Wilson grew up in turn, routed the way Chantel was raised. Like mother, like daughter.

At a house party at the tender age of fourteen, Ms. Wilson met a guy name Brian. He was her type; smooth talking, clean cut, hard body, kind of guy. They exchanged small talk before he pulled her over to the corner where the drinks were. They drank and danced in the corner under the dim light until she started losing concept of how hot it was and how much she was sweating her edges out.

"You ready to leave? This party's getting kind of wack," he yelled in her ear over the music.

"Yeah you're right. Can you give me a ride home?" she slurred out.

Her balance and coordination was way off at this point. In her hand she held loosely onto her fifth red plastic cup filled with the iconic party red punch saturated with Everclear.

He told her they should go to his house for a little while and then he promised to take her home. She didn't know any better because she was so intoxicated that she couldn't even walk out on her own. He held her up and opened his car door and helped her inside. She had no idea what she was getting herself into and wouldn't have any idea until she woke up the next day in his bed naked and violated.

Later she found out that he was actually twenty-one and that night he took her over to his house and raped her while she was barely even conscious. She had no idea what was even happening because all she wanted to do was close her eyes and sleep. The alcohol took over her mind and body, letting her fall limp to his easy access. After he did what he intended to do from the start of the night he didn't want anything to do with her. He wouldn't even drive her home; she had to catch a bus. Luckily she still had her life and health but she ended up pregnant and had no idea what to do.

She didn't tell anyone about this incident because she was embarrassed to tell anyone that she was taken advantage of. She had too much pride and a reputation to protect in her eyes. Her parents never even knew, and when they found out she was pregnant they kicked her out the house. No questions asked; they just made her leave. She struggled her way through her pregnancy on her own and lived from place to place, with friends or different guys she met. She became even more street smart because she needed the streets to survive and raise her baby. Nine months later, she was torn up inside because it was hard for her to accept the baby she named Chantel. She would always think about that night she was taken advantage of. She couldn't handle it emotionally and sometimes took it out on her daughter. Not really caring or even knowing how to raise a baby she made many mistakes. A short year later she gave birth to another baby, a son she named Chris. While Chantel was growing up she had to basically fend for herself just as her mother had too and on top of that she looked out for her younger brother. The cycle just continued.

Current day

Simone sat up startled from the yelling coming from outside her bedroom door. She blinked repeatedly trying to let her eyes adjust to the dark. The outline of her dresser, desk and chair came into vision. She peered down at the small amount of light streaming in under her door and listened.   The yelling got louder and louder and was followed by lots of movement. She flopped back down in bed with a loud sigh and pulled her baby blue comforter over her head in an attempt to at least muffle the loudness of her parents screams.

"Ughhh! I'm sick of this! Shut the hell up mom!" she yelled to herself under the blanket. She just knew it was something her mom was complaining about.

After laying there for ten minutes under her blanket in a failed attempt to fall back asleep she threw the blanket off her and stood up. Again taking a second to adjust to the darkness, she walked slowly to her door and pulled it open. The hallway light was on and across the hall her parent's bedroom door was closed. Hesitantly, Simone walked down the hall and stopped. She stood wiggling her toes in the fuzzy cream colored carpet, contemplating if she should interrupt. She concluded that she should and knocked. Silence.

"Dad?" she called through the door. More silence. She knocked again.

"Simone, go back to bed," a man's voiced answered.

"I can't sleep with you guys yelling."

A woman's voice snapped back, "Go to bed, Simone!"

Simone turned and started walking back to her room and almost immediately heard them again. She rolled her eyes, annoyed that they completely just ignored her request. She leaned on her door frame and stared back at her parent's room and listened.

"No… George, tell your daughter. Tell her what shit you've been doing. Let her know what daddy is doing!" her mother yelled with an emphasis on *daddy*. "Tell her where you're sticking you dick!"

"Would you just shut up!" he disgustingly said back.

"George, just give it up. Seriously. You're a fucking liar and I know it. Business trip? I talked to Mr. Carson and he told me that the trip was only one night. Why where you gone two nights? What were you doing? " she asked.

"I'm not going to keep going through this with you.   I'm not lying and I'm about fed up with trying to explain that to you. You are my wife, mother of my child and there's no way I would step outside of that. Damn!" he shot back, shaking his head in disbelief at his wife's accusations. "I'm surprised you even noticed I was gone."

Simone sighed and closed her door and got back in her bed. Thoughts of seeing her father with another woman ran through her head but she quickly shook the feeling. She couldn't believe her father would cheat. He was such a great father and husband, she just couldn't see it. Being a daddy's girl made her bias to the facts though. The idea that her father was cheating was just unbelievable and she wouldn't accept it. Her mother was the one to blame in her mind. She thought her mom was being unreasonable, extremely jealous and insecure for no reason. She just wished her mother would stop accusing him of cheating. He would never do that, she thought. Snuggled in her comforter she forced herself back to sleep.

The next morning she woke up to silence which was a pleasant thing to hear since last night. I hope my mom's out she thought as she rubbed the sleep out of her eyes. She picked up her cell phone, saw no missed calls and threw it back down on the bed. She slid her brown Old Navy flip flops on and walked out to the kitchen and realized both her parents were out early on a Saturday morning.

She made a bowl of cereal and flopped down on the soft black leather loveseat in the family room. Grabbed the remote control, turned to BET and watched Beyonce's *"Halo"* video as she devoured her Honey Nut Cheerios.   Interrupted by a few knocks, she put the bowl down on the coffee table and walked to the front door.

"Who is it?" she asked as she struggled to make out whose shape it was on the other side of the door through the peep hole.

"I'm looking for Mrs. Hayes. I have a delivery for her," the mystery voice answered.

Simone opened the door to greet the stranger with a smile. There was a short stubby white man standing there with what looked like a black toupee on his head covering the obvious massive bald spot that lay under it. The reading glasses he had on looked like they were about to slide all the way off his greasy nose. He wore a navy blue and white stripped button up shirt, with the top two buttons open, exposing a mop of grayish hair protruding out. The shirt was neatly tucked into his high water khaki pants and finished off with a pair of small brown penny loafers. He had a small utility belt on with a few black gadgets strapped in. She couldn't make out what they were though. Weird little man she thought.

"I'm her daughter, I can take it." She reached her hand out to take the envelope.

"Ok, well, make sure she gets these and no one else does. They are very important. Tell her a Mr. Haines dropped them off and to give me a call once she receives it," he said and nodded his head before walking off.

"Ok, sure," Simone closed the door and immediately looked over the envelope.

It was blank except the name Mrs. Hayes scribbled across the top right hand corner in blue ink. She curiously ran her fingers along the shape of whatever was inside but couldn't figure it out.

She dropped it on the kitchen table and went back to get her cereal bowl and washed it. Occupying the rest of her day was the next thought on her mind. She called one of her friends and made plans to go to the mall. Completely forgetting to make sure her mom got the envelope before she left to go shopping. They spent all day looking for something to wear to a house party that was going on that night. She ended up not finding anything and returned home a failure. She figured she would have to create an outfit from something she already owned.

Entering the house, she wondered why the lights were all out, but her mother's car was there. It was too early for her to be sleep; she thought back to when she checked the time in the car on the way home and it was only 7:20pm. She closed the door behind her and walked into something unknown. She looked down and realized she tripped over a big black object near the front door and almost fell but she caught her balance by grabbing the wall. She ran her hand along it, searching for the hallway light and flicked it on. There were bags, suitcases and boxes stacked along the hallway.

"Mom?" she confusingly called. But there was no response.

She walked into the kitchen, turned the light on and her attention was immediately drawn to the kitchen table. The envelope and its contents were sprawled randomly across the table. Pictures. She walked closer and saw her father holding, kissing and laughing with a woman. The shock of it made her grab the edge of the table. Her face became a mix of confusion, disgust, and disbelief as she picked up each picture one by one and saw the happiness of the couple at dinner. They were seated on the patio of a restaurant, with champagne glasses in hand in some of the photos, other times they were leaned across the table kissing.

The overwhelming feeling of betrayal took over as she searched through her purse for her cell phone. She knocked out half its contents as she pulled out her phone and dialed her father's number. He didn't answer and she called right back. Still no answer. She couldn't understand it. What did her mother do to make him do this, she thought? She just knew it was her mother's fault. She walked back through the hall way and realized that it was her father's stuff packed up. She saw his suits in garment bags, his shoes were all packed in two boxes and more of his clothes stuffed in duffle bags and suitcases. She was torn. She loved her father dearly and in no way wanted him to move out but she was angry at his actions that were causing him to have to leave her. When she made it to the end of the hallway, her mother's door was shut so she knocked softly.

"Mom?" she asked.

"Come in," her mother said.

She opened the door and saw her mother sitting up in her bed with the cream blanket up to her waist. She was leaning up against the back headboard with her head in her hands. The smell of vodka consumed her nostrils as she walked in. Her mother looked up at Simone with blood shot red eyes, then turned away and stared out the window.

"Mom, I saw the pictures," she paused. "What happened?" Simone asked timidly.

Her mother continued to stare out the window and then took a sip of her vodka from a black mug that sat on the night stand. She inhaled deeply after the warmth traveled down her throat, through her chest and settled in her stomach.

She wiped at a tear that ran down her cheek. "You see what kind of person your dad is. He's not a man. Don't you ever put everything into a man. Ever. They ain't shit. Thank God, I got my own. He is gone."

2

~ West Side ~

Later that year

The flight to California was long; too long. Simone sat in the grey plastic cushioned chair, leaned forward holding her head. She could just hear a bed calling her name through the hustle of the commuting airline passengers, kids crying for their mothers, and suitcases rolling along the marble floors. Her mind wandered to what she would do with her time in California. No friends, no job, no fun. *Oh well, as long as I'm away from my annoying mother I don't even care,* she thought. For the fifth time in a row, she checked the time on her cell phone. "Come on dad," she moaned to herself. Just then her cell phone rang.

"Hello," Simone said as she answered her phone with a slight annoyance in her voice.

"Did your dad get you yet?" her mother asked.

"No. I'm in the waiting area. He needs to hurry up, I'm tired. I couldn't sleep on the plane."

"Call him again."

"Oh. Wait he's calling me now actually. Bye." She pulled the phone from her ear and pushed a button. She whined in the phone, "Dad, where are you?"

"I'm sitting outside, you said Delta, right?" He said as he scanned his surroundings.

"Yes." She stood up and looked out the window. "I see you, stay there."

She hung up, grabbed her two rolling suitcases, duffle bag and struggled to walk over to her dad, occasionally tripping on the wheels. When she got out the door, he got out to greet her.

He reached out and hugged her but she didn't hug back. Her hands were full and she hardly had her balance. She smiled a little as he took two of her bags. He had on a grey sweat suit that fit a little to snug for her taste and a pair of running sneakers. He looked way more casual than usual. Simone was accustomed to seeing her dad in shirts and ties but this was the first time she has seen him since her mother put him out.

"How was the flight?" he asked as they began to walk towards the car.

"Good," she said flatly.

"Did you sleep?" he asked.

"No."

They walked to the back of the car in an awkward silence. He popped the trunk of his white Acura and threw her bags inside.

"So... How is your mom doing?" he asked as they glanced at each other from opposite sides of the car. She got in the passenger side without answering, he followed.

"You gonna answer me?" he asked as he checked his rear view mirror and pulled off.

"She's fine," Simone answered, glaring out the window at the passing cars.

The once happy and close knit relationship the two shared was slightly tattered. Her father tried his best to continue to be normal but Simone just wasn't able to accept what her father did. How could he betray their family she wondered?

They drove down a long stretch of highway until exiting. She shifted her feet uncomfortably getting tired of the car ride. There was a red and black club that lay near her feet and she moved to avoid stepping on it. Out the window a group of young kids ran chasing each other around in circles down the sidewalk, and a woman dressed in a long dingy t-shirt, stone washed shorts, and hair that seemed to have never seen a comb ever, slowly walked up the street talking to herself. Every other corner had a liquor store or a corner store swarmed with people in and out. The only grass she saw anywhere was never cut low and full of weeds. The houses were smaller then what she was used to and hardly had a yard. The paint peeled off most, and some were completely boarded up. She was not used to this type of environment at all. Born and raised in the suburbs, this was shocking to see. She only saw this type of thing on TV or in movies.

The area that they drove in she prayed was just somewhere they had to pass through to get to his house. It wasn't. They parked in front of an apartment building that looked about twenty floors high. There was a cement fixture in the front that was filled with dirt, she assumed for a garden but nothing was growing. There were a few broken bottles lying in the dirt though. Across the street was a fenced off basketball court and she glanced over at the boys playing. Most of them had no shirts on and the sweat glistened off their chests as the glaring sun beat down on them. At least there was one good sight to see she thought to herself.

In the elevator she held her breath so the stench of urine didn't invade her nose. On the ninth floor they exited the elevator and walked down a winding hallway. The floor was a cream and light grey colored surface full of scuff marks and the walls were a similar cream color painted over large cement bricks. An old wrinkled woman pushing a walker slowly made her way past them towards the elevator as they made their way to room 917.

"Well, here is your summer home," he said with a smile and stuck his key inside the hole. They walked in and she stood in the living room taking in her surroundings. I can't stay here she thought as the little bit of positive spirit she had about the trip was drained from her.

"I have an extra room that I cleared out for you. There's just a bed. No other furniture at this point but I will work on that. There is a TV out here in the living room, and the kitchen is right there, the bathroom is that door right there," he said pointing to the left then to the right.

He grabbed her bags and dragged them to her empty room. She walked in and plopped exhaustedly on the bed and inhaled then exhaled deeply. The walls were the same large cement bricks from the hallways but were painted white. The floor was covered with a dirty orange carpet that was frayed at the door entrance. There was a mini closet to her right filled with a handful of lonely wire hangers. She reached around behind her to lift the small window but it was stuck. She turned around and got on her knees on the bed and tried again. It finally gave and opened.

Simone couldn't believe she had to spend her summer in this dirt box with her father. She wanted to go home already; she missed her room, her bed, her TV, and her friends, but definitely not her mother. She lay down cautiously on the bed, unsure of what or who laid there before her and fell asleep. The next day she decided she had to do something with her time other then stare at the cement walls of her room. It made her feel like she was on punishment, so she asked to borrow her father's car to go to a mall. He was hesitant to let her go for fear of her getting lost but he was confident in her driving since she has had her license for a little over a year. He gave her keys, directions and told her to fill out some job applications while she was there. The thought of working a job made her chuckle to herself. There was no way in hell she was going to get a job; she would just call her mom for money.

This was the day Simone's life was going to change. She walked into Bakers shoe store and was followed by a girl who looked to be about the same age of seventeen. She was a little browner skinned then Simone and had thick dark brown hair. She wore big gold bamboo earrings, a white tank top, fitted dark blue jeans, a pair of black and white Jordans and carried a big camel color leather purse. It was Chantel but Simone had yet to find that out.

Simone saw a pair of black strappy shoes that she fell in love with instantly and asked the petite saleswoman for an eight and a half, then took a seat on the bench in the middle of the store. The woman bought the shoes back to her and she tried them on. She stood up and eyed how they looked then walked across the small store to make sure she could walk comfortably in them.

"Those are cute on you," the girl said and pointed to Simone's feet.

"Thanks. I think I like them too," she answered.

She walked over to the mirror, turned to the side and pulled her jeans up to get a better view. She took a minute to admire her creamy caramel complexion, long dark black hair, extremely long eye lashes around her oval eyes, her high cheek bones, and her pouty full lips. Then ran her eyes down her body taking a second to appreciate her full C breast, thin waist, and curvy hips, down to her pretty little toes that sat perfectly in the black strappy shoes. *Damn, I look good* she thought to herself. She decided she was going to get them so she sat down and began taking them off.

Chantel asked the petite saleswoman for the same shoe in an eight. "I think I want them too, now," Chantel laughed out.

The woman returned and handed Chantel the shoes then walked over to the desk to ring up Simone. After Simone paid, she turned to walk out but noticed a pair of red pumps. *Damn you can't ever leave the store with one thing*, she thought to herself. She walked over to the shoes, picked them up, checked the price and debated trying them on. They were a little out of her price range.

Chantel called over the same petite saleswoman who was near the back where the shoes were, to bring her a size eight and a half instead. As soon as the woman went in the back to get the next size up, Chantel stuffed the size eights in her huge purse and quickly walked out. Simone stood there looking dumb for a minute. In shock of what she just saw, she realized she should leave too before the saleswoman questions her. She didn't want to be a snitch so she put the red shoe down and walked as fast as she could into the closest store, and noticed the same girl in that store. *Damn, she's bold*, Simone thought.

Simone went back to her shopping, looking through a table of jeans for her size. She didn't find her size and gave up, and moved on to the accessories section. She noticed the same girl was going in and out of the dressing room, trying on clothes. She wondered if she was really planning on buying them or pulling the same stunt she just did in the previous store. A man dressed in blue jeans and a black t-shirt stood across the store staring at Chantel. He didn't look like he was dressed in any kind of uniform but he sure looked like he was watching her. *Damn, she is going to get caught*, Simone thought. The idea of going to tell her she was being watched crossed her mind but she didn't want to get involved. It would look like she was part of the plan and if the girl got caught they would try to take her down too. Damn, she pondered.

Chantel finished with whatever scheme she was involved in and began to walk to the exit of the store. Simone looked back and noticed the man in the black shirt began to walk towards the door also. He picked up his pace to a slight jog as Chantel walked out the door. Simone jumped in front of the man in the black shirt before he could get out the store to chase her and played the role of her life. She deserved an Oscar for this one.

"Uhh…can…I use…your…phone?" She struggled to get the question out and grabbed the man by the shoulder. He looked at her like she was crazy and continued to try to get around her but she jumped in his way each time.

"I need…my inhaler…I can't breathe!" she wheezed out.

His eyes bulged out when he realized that she was having an asthma attack. He reached down and grabbed his cell phone out the clip and handed it to her. She dialed her own cell number, remembering that it was on silent. She began talking into the voicemail to throw him off.

"Mom…what store are you in?" she wheezed out and turned around and looked out the store to make sure the girl was out of distance.

The man was getting impatient and was leaning outside the store looking around but he didn't want to leave his phone with a stranger. She hung up and handed back the phone and quickly walked out. He ran out to the middle of the hall in the mall and stood looking around for the girl. He realized he lost her and slowly walked back defeated, to his store.

Simone figured that was enough excitement for the day and decided to leave.   On the way back to her dad's car, she noticed the same girl crossing the street, walking towards the bus stop. Something about this girl just drew Simone in and intrigued her so she offered to give her a ride home.   She found out she lived right around the corner from her dad's apartment complex.   This was the beginning of a friendship like no other.

3

~ Hood Mentality ~

The two became inseparable. Where you saw Chantel you would see Simone. Simone knew this was going to be an exciting summer on the west coast for her. They spent most of their time over Chantel's apartment because Ms. Wilson, Chantel's mother, was never around, giving them the space and opportunity to do whatever they wanted. They also spent a lot of time around Chantel's younger brother, Chris, and his friends.

Chris was only a year younger than Chantel but anyone who didn't really know them well would never know that. People thought he was older than Chantel because of the lifestyle he lived and the mindset he had. He was making big money by hustling all night every night. He was making a name for himself, and had the respect of older guys around the neighborhood while his peers feared him. He was smart though and never got caught up. He did what he had to do and everyone knew better then to cross him. Chris never even had to handle anything on his own, he ran with a crew that was down for him no matter what. So Chantel was well taken care of as well, by her brother and his boys. The streets welcomed these two with open arms; it was the only home they knew.

Growing up Chantel became a master thief. At fifteen, she started with robbing stores but when she got all the clothes, shoes and jewelry she needed she started robbing guys that she gamed up. By the time she was seventeen, she looked like money wherever she went, and that attracted everyone's attention. She always turned heads and had every man after her, so that left her with the power to have her pick. She went for the ballers and money makers because she always had an agenda…to get that paper.

16

Her biggest pay days were from some sucker named T. He was the cockiest dude she ever met and she hated him but she played her part well. Get in where you fit in was her motto. She met him at a party, and not just any party. This party was for the best of the best and the biggest of the biggest. Of course she had her fake ID ready. She went with her new found friend, Simone, who was down for the plans too. They both worked these guys and were good at it. Chantel had the upper hand because she had the gift of gab, charisma for days and she was the one who turned Simone on to it. They both were extraordinarily beautiful. Even though the summer just started and they just became friends, Simone was catching on quickly.

Chantel had on black stilettos with a fresh pedicure. She had on a short tight black dress that showed off her curvy figure. She had on all diamond and platinum jewelry that had her neck, ears, wrist and fingers looking like they belong in a freezer. Of course it was real too, either a product of a robbery or a gift from a guy. She was turning heads as soon as she walked in. No one was fucking with her that night. When they walked in they scanned the room and found a spot at the bar to chill for a minute. They took their time to find the big money, because they only worked the best. They didn't have time for small time hustlers running shit for the big dogs. They wanted the top man. The desperate and weak ones always approached first and as sure as they thought they would, they did.

Two small time runners came up to them. "Can we get you two drinks?" the shorter one asked.

Before they even spoke back they checked out the clothes, because that was always a sure way to tell who is on what level. They were wearing some expensive clothes, shoes and had lots of big jewelry hanging from their necks and wrist. They looked like they were trying to flaunt it so hard, Chantel thought. Just on that note alone, Chantel realized they would probably be cocky and hand out money like it was water. She decided to take the offer for drinks.

"So what's your name?" one guy asked Simone as he put his arm around her waist.

"My name is Simone, and if you don't mind I would rather you not touch me," she said and slide out his grip. She was playing hard to get.

"Oh, my bad, ma, I'm just a friendly dude. Feel me? And my name is Ron by the way and this is my boy T," he answered and smiled. His boy nodded his head to them.

While Simone talked to Ron, the other guy, T, was paying for the drinks. He pulled out his money to pay and Chantel checked his stash out. It was big but she never heard of these guys before, so she was still distant because she didn't know what level they were on. They just seemed so anxious, but that might be better because when they are young minds in the game that meant they usually were stupid. So Chantel decided to try her luck on them, she usually didn't step to them this early, but she had a feeling this was going to be easy money. They drank their drinks and flirted a little to show their interest.

"Yo, what's good for after this?" Chantel asked T as she stood up close to his face and rubbed her body against his lightly.

She smelled of peaches and that made him think of tasting her. He got excited with the touch of her body and all he could do was smile. Simone saw that Chantel planned on sticking with these guys so she follower her lead. Simone had on a low cut top that showed off her size full C breast. She leaned down to scratch and imaginary itch near her ankle letting her breast hang out even more. Ron just stared in lust at her and took the last gulp of his drink.

"We can go back to my place and have the after party there, is that ok with you two ladies?" T asked with a grin. He pulled out his car keys that were on a Benz key chain, dangled it in the air and said he would drive.

They didn't mind because they got dropped off by Chantel's brother. Chantel laughed in her head as they got into the brand new Benz that T drove. She knew it was going to be an easy night. They didn't even sleep with the dudes and got about three-hundred a piece for just chillin with them. They just teased them all night, made them believe they would eventually get some. Chantel and Simone figured out these guys had major paper and had to keep them for the long run. They decided to stay in touch with them and throughout the three months of the summer that Simone was in California, these girls got money, clothes, jewelry, paid trips, and Chantel even got a car out the deal. When they got bored they just cut them off, and put word on the street that Chantel's brother was not feeling them trying to talk to his sister. The streets were talking and Ron and T were sure as hell listening because they were not after Chantel and Simone anymore out of respect for Chris.

Chris and Chantel loved the life they were living but knew it wouldn't last forever. They knew they had to get out before their life that was up, would eventually come down. So whatever they got, they made sure to save so they could move out the hood and take their mother with them. They were too smart to think this lifestyle would last for long.

Chantel kept her games up for a long time, getting whatever she needed. Chantel's mother, Ms. Wilson, never questioned where she got her stuff from because she was too busy getting high. Ms. Wilson long lost the beautiful looks that carried her through her teen years, and now was a sickly looking woman with blotchy and too early wrinkled skin. Her once luscious honey blonde hair has long changed to a damaged, dry and broken, yellowish color and her youthful hazel eyes now screamed a scorned, painful life. Chantel tried numerous times to get her mom to stop taking drugs and get her life together, but her mother wasn't trying to hear it. Chris was so embarrassed of his mother's habit that he stopped even associating with her in public. Their mother was on the streets passing tricks for drugs or money to buy drugs. She would have to go out of the neighborhood to get her fix because no one around the way would serve her because they knew who she was. They hated to see their mom turned out by the very substance that feed their mouths. There wasn't anything they could do because she was so deep into the habit. They couldn't stop her and got tired of trying. She would even try to steal from Chantel and Chris. They had to keep their money and anything valuable away from her.

Their mother spent a lot of time with her boyfriend, Jonathan, who was also on drugs. He was a tall skinny man; skinny to the point where he looked unhealthy, most likely because of the drugs. He was brown skinned with black hair that almost looked like dreads were beginning to form. He had a long jagged scar down the right side of his face that was a constant reminder of a fight he encountered on the streets once. Ms. Wilson and he spent majority of the day trying to figure where they were going get their next fix and when they weren't getting high they were busy trying to hustle up some money for their next hit. Ms. Wilson tried to hold jobs, but was constantly getting fired. She either got caught stealing or was high at work. She bounced from job to job and was at an all time low, unable to get another one. Jonathan moved in with them a year ago and was in the same predicament as Ms. Wilson. He was no help to the bills or any of the responsibilities of the house. Only thing he as good for was keeping Ms. Wilson happy and helping her with her habit.

Although Ms. Wilson was busying trying to get high, she was still a mother and tried to be there when she could. She loved her kids but the temptation just took over. She knew her kids were smart, and knew how to handle themselves, so she didn't worry too much about them. Plus they basically took care of her even though they were only sixteen and seventeen years old. One night the roles reversed and Chantel would need some taking care of.

4

~ Trust No One ~

Ms. Wilson rolled over, awakened by the ring of her phone. "Hello?" She answered, wiping the sleep out of her eye. Who in the hell is calling my house at three in the damn morning she thought as she sat up in her bed.

"Mrs. Wilson? This is Officer Johnson," the voice on the other line answered.

"Yes," she replied and rolled her eyes expecting it to be her boyfriend or son getting into more trouble like always.

"Your daughter is in St. John's hospital, she was raped tonight. We need you to come to the hospital right away," the officer said with no pity in his voice. This type of thing happened often in their city. These kinds of calls were routine.

"What! Is she ok? What happened?" Ms. Wilson screamed through the phone as if it was the officer's fault.

"Ma'm, we can't give you any information like that over the phone, but she is ok. Just come down immediately," he said and they hung up.

She rolled out of bed still sleepy, threw on a pair of grey sweat pants, a dingy t-shirt without a bra and her sneakers. When she got to the hospital she went to the front desk and asked where she could find her daughter. She was directed to the waiting room where they said the doctors would contact her. She sat in the cold white chair and waited. Every possible thought went through her mind as she anxiously waited to find out how her daughter was and what happened. She nervously tapped her foot and fiddled with her finger nails. She knew it was her fault for letting her daughter run the streets at all times of the night. For the first time, the overwhelming feeling of guilt and responsibility took over her sober at the time mind. She knew she should have been more on top of where her daughter was and who she was with.

She pulled out her outdated prepaid cell phone and called her son, Chris, telling him what happened and to come down to the hospital. He was heated and said he would be there as soon as he could. She then called Jonathan who didn't come home that night. He stayed with her most nights but was missing a lot of others; it wasn't unusual. Chantel and Chris got along well with him because he was around for the longest. Besides the drugs and stealing, they thought he was an ok guy. Usually their mom had different guys in and out but this one seemed to be consistent for about a year. They got used to him and called him Jay for short instead of Jonathon. His phone just rang and rang but she never got through to him so she left a message; told him what happened and where she was. The hospital was pretty crowded because it was a hot summer Saturday night and everyone was getting into something, and causing problems. She had nothing to do but sit and wait for word on her daughter.

At the hospital the doctor finally came out to Chantel's mother and approached her. She stood up and was scared to even speak. The tension in her body and the anticipation of seeing her daughter gave her a headache. The doctor told her to walk with him and he explained to her that Chantel was raped but that she is ok. He told her that she has a few scratches and bruises but nothing too serious. The doctor explain that she would need to come back soon for another pregnancy, STD and HIV test because the rapist didn't use a condom and there is no telling what could have been passed this early. When she got to Chantel's room there was a young male, blonde headed police officer concluding the questioning. She walked over to the bed and looked over her daughter who was beat up badly in the face. Tiny red lines ran through the whites of Ms. Wilson's eyes as tears began to drip down. She not only felt for her daughter but she thought back to when she was raped and the hell it caused her life. She hugged her daughter gently while trying not to hurt her. Chantel laid there without a tear in her eye, only anger in her heart. She was not sad one bit; only anger consumed her.

"Ms. Wilson, I need to speak to you outside please," the young blonde officer said and pointed toward the door. She squeezed her daughters hand tightly and slowly walked away not taking her eyes off her until she got to the door.

"Ma'am, your boyfriend, Jonathan Kempt, is being accused of

this rape against your daughter. He is being held and since Chantel is only seventeen and in the hospital we are required by law to press charges whether you want to or not," the officer said and handed her some papers she had to sign.

Ms. Wilson took a step back, "Wait...Jonathan?" She said, "Jonathan did this to her?" she questioned as she ran her hands through her hair and bit her bottom lip in anger and confusion.

"Yes Ma'am," the blonde officer answered while still holding the papers out.

"Are you sure? Is she drugged or anything? Does the story make sense? Can you ask her again," she demanded.

"Ma'am we went over the story three times and she has made it clear that a Mr. Jonathan Kempt did this to her."

"No...No. I don't believe it," she said calmly, shaking her head. "There is a mistake. She must be lying. Let me go ask her." She opened the door but the officer grabbed it.

"Ma'am. We already have her statement and a rape kit was performed. DNA will determine truth from lie."

She stood still staring at the shiny yellowish linoleum floor with the image of Jonathan on top of Chantel replaying over and over in her mind. She fell back against the wall and her face scrunched up. "Why?" she mumbled to herself as tasted the salty tears that flowed from her eyes, down her cheeks, dripped past her mouth and off her chin. She slid down the wall with her head in her hands and grabbed handfuls of her hair on each side.

"What did she say? What happened?" she said as she lifted her head and peeked up at the officer from the ground. He began to give a rundown of her night that led up to the rape.

"Chantel went out with Simone around 7pm and asked to be dropped off at a male friend's house. His name is Anthony." The officer asked, "Are you familiar with that name?"

Ms. Wilson nodded her head yes, "I think that's her boyfriend."

The officer continued.

Earlier that night

Chantel knocked on the door but got no answer at first. So she knocked even harder...

"Who is it?" he yelled through the door

"It's Chantel, open the door, Ant!" Chantel yelled back as she stared at the old wooden door that was an invitation for splinters.

There was a few seconds of dead silence. Then he started to unlock the door and opened it. She stepped inside the door frame and he grabbed her, stopping her. He wrapped his arms around her tightly and pulled away, ending with a kiss.

"What's that for?" she asked with a big grin on her face.

"Just wanted to kiss you, can I just want to kiss u? Damn, baby," he said as he continued to hold her.

"Well you going to let me in or what?" she asked and slide out his arms and pushed him lightly.

"I'm actually about to go out, I didn't know you were coming by," he said

"You ain't even dressed; you got on a wife beater and boxers. There's something I want from you before you leave."

Chantel grinned and grabbed his dick through his boxers. He jumped back, smiled and grabbed his own stuff. He blushed.

"Baby, why you gotta do this to me, I really have to go," he said as he backed up a little from her temptation.

She stepped in more and closed the door behind her. She kissed him and went from his mouth, to his neck while pressing her body against his. He started squirming because he wanted her to stop but it was feeling too good. She reached in his boxers and grabbed his dick and massaged it and it had him open for anything. He forgot he wanted her to leave in the first place and his mind was solely on the tingling in his boxers. She got on her knees and pulled it out and went to work. His mind was all fucked up; head was back and eyes closed. He grabbed her head and guided himself in and out her mouth. He moaned softly from the pleasure she was bringing him. He loved every minute of it. When he opened his eyes to watch her head bob up and down he came back to reality. His attention was immediately drawn to the girl standing in the living room watching with her arms crossed across her chest. He thought he could get away with it, but was mistaken.

"Oh, shit!" he yelled, stumbled back and pulled up his boxers, leaving Chantel there on her knees confused.

Chantel looked up and saw a girl standing there in a long white t-shirt and it appeared she had nothing on under it. She almost lost her mind that very second.

"Oh, hell no!" Chantel yelled and jumped up.

She began swinging wildly getting at least three good hits to his face before he could restrain her. The girl disappeared in the darkness in the living room and returned with her clothes on and purse in hand. Anthony struggled trying to contain Chantel but she was determined to finish hitting him until she was satisfied.

"Chantel! Come on, stop!" he yelled at her as he tried to carry her to the front door. "You have to get the fuck out with all this."

"Fuck you! Forreal, Ant, you got some bitch in here? You ain't shit!" she screamed and clawed at his face.

"Ant, I can't believe you," the anonymous girl said softly. "I'm sorry, I didn't know he had a girlfriend or anything. I'm out."

The girl tried to walk past them out the door but Chantel was still wildly flinging her arms around trying to hit him. Chantel grilled the girl and tried to calm herself down.

"Ant, put me down. I'm done." She stopped struggling and held her hands up as if to imply she was finished. "Listen, I don't want his sorry ass. You can have him."

She looked from the girl to him, staring coldly in his eyes. He slowly loosened his grip and she pushed him off her.

"Fuck you, Ant," Chantel said, slamming the door behind her.

She stood on the sidewalk realizing she didn't have a ride home. She pulled out her cell phone and called her brother to see if he was available to pick her up but he was over an hour away. Their mother's car broke down a few days ago and she was in no hurry to get it fixed, so it now sits on the street in front of their house. Chris said he would pay to get it fixed when she secured a job. He was getting tired of her asking for gas money almost every day anyway. She called Simone but she didn't answer. So her last resort was Jay. He said he would be there in about ten minutes. As she waited, she ran her house key across the side of Ant's car and laughed to herself.

Jay pulled up in his old raggedy '99 Toyota Corolla and Chantel climbed in the passenger side. She inhaled a powerful trace of alcohol lingering on Jay. He must have been drinking she thought. As he drove she paid close attention to his driving judgment and he didn't seem to be too impaired, so she relaxed a bit. She called Simone again and this time she answered. She ran through the details of what just happened nonstop, only pausing to hear an occasional 'What!' or 'No he didn't!' on the other end.

Jay pulled over to a dark side street and Simone eyed her surroundings cautiously. There weren't any people around and the houses on the block were either uninhibited or had no lights on. The street light was a dim fluorescent that barely reached the ground below. It appeared to be a dead end as far as she could see.

"Simone, let me call you back," Chantel said tentatively into her cell phone. She closed it and placed it in her purse. "Where are we?"

"I gotta pick up something for your mom," he said staring off into the distance. His mind was relaxed from the Hennessy he drank a little earlier.

Simone sucked her teeth but was used to the routine. She locked her car door, squirmed in her seat as she tried to pull down her mini jean skirt a little and leaned back to get a little more comfortable. A couple minutes of silence past. Jay looked at Chantel out the side of his eye. He fingered the toothpick that hung out the corner of his mouth with his slimy pink tongue as thoughts of sin ran through his head. He reached his scrawny hand out and ran it up her thigh. Simone immediately brushed his hand off and leaned up against the door. "What are you doing?" she yelled in disgust.

He tried again, but this time he reached up her jean skirt with one hand and the other one he grabbed her breast. She squirmed in her seat and tried to push his hands off her as she yelled at him to stop. He wouldn't stop though. She reached for the door but he punched her in the face, which was a little too much for her to handle. He was a grown man with a heavy hand. She couldn't believe what was going on and was a little in shock. She tried to get out the car again but he grabbed her hands trying to hold her down.

With one of his hands he held her hands together and tried to pull her laced pink thong off with his other. She was struggling and squirming around to keep her legs closed and her underwear on. He got them half way down her thighs when she got one hand lose and hit him in the face repeatedly, screaming for help. No one heard her, because no one was around the dark street. Her hits didn't hurt him as much as they just annoyed him so he punched her in the face again to get her to stop fussing. He busted her bottom lip and blood trickled down her chin.

She continued to attempt to keep her legs closed and somehow managed to get out his grip and open the door. As she was halfway out he grabbed her by the waist and pulled her forcefully back into the car, making her head bang back on the top of door frame. She fell back lifelessly into the passenger seat.

She was knocked unconscious. Satisfied that the struggle was over, he got out and walked to her side of the car and pulled her out. He placed her on the front hood of his car and stood there staring at her beautiful body that he always secretly admired and wanted for himself. He rubbed her breast through her purple tank top, and then pulled her shirt up to look at them. He pulled off her skirt and underwear and just stared at her beauty. He was growing more and more excited and couldn't wait anymore. He forced it inside her because she was not inviting. He fucked her on top of the car hood, then pulled out, and then turned her over so he could enter from the back. He got back inside her and finished. When he was done he laid her over in a corner of the alley and drove off, leaving her there for someone to find her naked and beat up. Alcohol was a hell of a drug to make Jay act so irrationally.

As the blonde hair officer finished up the story, Chris arrived. He saw the pain in his mother's eyes and stopped dead in his tracks.

"Yo, where she at?" he questioned. She motioned to the door behind her. She stopped him before he entered the room.

"Jay did this to her," Ms. Wilson said as she held him by the shoulders.

"What!" He yelled back, throwing her arms off him. "Your boyfriend Jay?" he questioned his mother with an anger like no other.

"That's what she is telling the police. I can't believe that shit," she said shaking her head.

"Aw, I'm going to get his ass," Chris said and paced back and forth. "Jay! Nah, Jay" he spoke to himself.

He walked into the room, up to the bed, held his sisters hand and gave her a kiss on the cheek.

"Yo, I'm going to handle this for you. I promise you that," he said to her and tried to fight back the tears. He kissed her again and walked out angry. He didn't even say anything else to his mom he just left.

Chantel was released from the hospital the next day. Ms. Wilson didn't really even try to take care of her because she was so stressed and upset about the situation that her drug habit got even worse. It was nearing the end of the summer so Simone was still around to be there for her. Although Chantel felt sick about the whole situation, she had no choice but to accept it. Word was all over the street about what happened and everyone was really pissed off about it. Chantel was like everyone's little sister around the neighborhood and everyone looked out for her. Chris was more angry then anyone and was ready to see Jay on the streets somewhere. He was out on bail until the trial and had nowhere to stay and they still had all his belongings. He was lucky for a while and kept out of dangers way until one night his luck just ran out.

Chris was out driving when he stopped at a red light. He couldn't believe he just happen to see Jay walking down the street. After all these nights of searching, he came across him so easy. He pulled over at the next corner and got out. He crept up behind him and smashed him on the back of the head with his gun. Jay fell to the ground holding his head and moaned out.

"Yeah, get yo bitch ass up now!" Chris said as he pointed his gun at Jay. Jay tried to focus and when he realized what was going on he pleaded with Chris to put the gun down. Feeling intoxicated with power because this was the first time he held his gun at a man with intentions of using it, Chris' heart pounded up and down.

"If you don't get up now I will waste your ass right here," Chris said still pointing the gun at him.

"Alright I'm getting up just don't shot me man," Jay pleaded as he staggered and stood up.

"Now walk yo ass right over there, we got some things to discuss." Chris said and pointed to around the corner. There weren't many lights so he nervously looked around to see if anyone saw him. His palms got sweaty as he gripped the gun and switched it back and forth in each hand, but still making sure to keep it pointed at him. He paced around Jay.

Jay knew what was up, but didn't have much of a choice, he just pleaded with Chris to let him go, kept saying sorry and that he was drunk when it happened. Chris wasn't hearing any of it, he was just seeing red. Anger. When they got to the side of the building that was on that block, he told Jay to get on his knees. Jay followed his orders.

"You know you fucked up, right?" Chris asked as he looked over his shoulder repeatedly.

"You gonna fuck with Chantel? Do you know who the fuck that girl is? That's my sister, my life right there. I live for her! When you made the decision to do that you made the decision to end your life," Chris said and pulled the trigger, not even giving Jay a chance to plead anymore.

His body fell limp to the ground while Chris stood over him and looked down with disgust. He looked around and stepped back slowly. He realized what he just did and made moves. He ran to his car and drove home as fast as he could. When he got home he ran inside and went straight to Chantel.

"Yo, I ended that for you," Chris said still holding the gun. His adrenaline was pumping and he didn't even think to put it somewhere. He was breathing in and out heavily.

"What?" Chantel screamed, jumped up and grabbed her brother. "Boy, what you do? Damn, we told you to leave it up to the law, Chris! You gonna have the cops after you now!" Chantel screamed and shook her brother by the shoulders. Their mother over heard what was going on and ran into the room and screamed at him, asking what happened.

"Yo, we out then. We leaving, start packing." He said and was dead serious. He paced the living room floor back and forth looking like he had no idea what he was going to do.

Simone came out the bathroom and closed the door. She curiously looked at Chantel as she used her jeans as a paper towel and rubbed her hands dry up and down her thighs. She could hear all the excitement going on when she was in the bathroom but didn't make out any specifics or words.

Chris stared at Simone. Ms. Wilson stared at Simone. Chanel stared at Simone. Simone looked from Chantel, to Chris to Ms. Wilson with a look of confusion. Chris broke the stare when he realized he was still holding his gun and quickly tucked it in his jeans and pulled his shirt over it.

"Um…is everything ok?" Simone questioned nervously.

"Yeah," Chantel said and walked over towards Simone. She eyed her mother and brother and nodded her head as if to signal that everything was ok. "Chris is in some trouble. So we have to figure out what the fuck to do." She cut her eye at Chris.

"Listen there isn't anything to figure out. Just pack your shit, we leaving," he said and pulled out his cell phone.

"Where are we going to go? We can't just get up and leave," Chantel yelled.

"Don't worry about it. I planned on leaving soon anyway; this is just a little more motivation. Just pack. If anyone comes looking for me, just say you haven't seen me since this morning," he said and walked out.

He had to pass his duties off to his boys. Everyone knew he planned on leaving soon but had no idea it would happen this way. Chantel stood staring at the door. Not sure what the plan was or what was going to happen, she felt out of control. She knew her brother usually had things under control but this was major. It was going to be hard to get out of this one and she had no clue what he was planning on doing. All she could do was trust him and start packing. Chantel and Ms. Wilson spent the next hour and a half packing up all of their belongings and Simone helped get Chris' stuff together.

Two hours went by and Chris finally showed back up. After he handled all his business in the street, picked up all his money that he stashed away, he brain stormed with his best friend Reese. Reese has been Chris's closest friend since they were little kids.   He also developed a summer time fling with Simone, so he suggested they move out to where Simone is from.

"Just get away from everything and tell no one," Reese said. "You know I got you."

Reese even gave him some cash to add to his savings to help them get into a house out there and be alright until he could figure things all the way out. To the East Coast they went.

5

~ East Side ~

Getting settled didn't take long. They found an apartment complex about ten minutes away from the town Simone lived in. The plan was to try to lead a normal life in the suburbs until they could come up with a more permanent plan. When they pulled up to their destination, Chantel immediately noticed there were no drug dealers on the corners, which were a permanent fixture in her old neighborhood. That was a clear sign that things would be different. There were front and back yards with fresh cut green grass. No liquor stores on every block, less people outside, you could even catch a squirrel run across a yard every now and then. She knew this would be a big change for her and her family but she was ready.

Chris just stayed low, trying to figure out what the next move for his life would be. He wasn't even thinking about enrolling in school or getting a job. He couldn't put his name down on any paper. He knew the drug game wasn't going to be as lucrative in this area also so he wasn't sure what he was going to do. Their mother had the biggest issue because she was no longer able to get the drugs she was used to getting and the loss of Jay was hard on her. Her health was in a horrible condition because the withdrawal effects and it was difficult for her to deal with. Chris, Chantel and Simone all helped her deal with it and did their best to take care of her. Their biggest challenge was to make sure that she didn't fall back into old habits.

Chantel was scared to enroll in school also for fear that they would link her to her brother and find out where they were. So Simone started her last year of High School but Chantel just couldn't go back. She didn't think it was that important anyway. Although it was an adjustment for all of them, things were going good. Eventually everyone was back to normal, adjusting to their surrounds and new life. Every aspect of their life had a complete turnaround compared to what they were used too. Luckily Chantel didn't suffer any long term effects from the rape just another blow to her heart. She was grateful to be out of her old neighborhood, away from drugs, crackheads, and a life full of sin. She missed the easy money, clothes and jewelry but she knew that she would eventually have to stop anyway.

Life was so good and Chantel was happy with everything, until the day she lost her brother. She prayed every night that it would never happen but this one morning, God couldn't answer her prayer. There were a ton of red and blue lights flaring outside of their apartment building and the police came banging on the door with a warrant of arrest for the murder of Jonathan Kempt. Strapped with huge guns and protected with bullet proof vest they invaded their apartment like an army of ants. Chantel stood there speechless as she watched them hand cuff her brother, drag him out and place him in the back of the police car. She didn't even have words to speak. She felt the life drained out of her. She couldn't even cry. Just stood there and watched with a blank face. Her brothers' eyes never left hers until he got in the car. They knew that was it. He wouldn't be coming back home.

"I don't know what to do. What do I do without my brother?" Simone said staring at the ground. She shifted her weight on her other leg and leaned back on the pillow on the couch.

"He will be back. Don't worry so much. You're going to drive yourself crazy," Simone tried to comfort her.

"He is NOT coming back. He's guilty and the best lawyer on this earth couldn't get him off. They have all the evidence they need," she paused. "I talked to him yesterday. He called and told me to not think about him. To make sure I figure out where I'm going to get money from since he is away. He just wants me to be strong and make sure I'm ok."

She ran her hands over her face as if to wipe away her problems. "He doesn't even seem to be phased about being in there." She sighed and shook her head.

"Well," Simone started. "You know your brother is strong. I guess the only thing we can do for him is make sure YOUR good so he doesn't have to worry about you also, you know."

"Yeah, I don't want him worried about me or mom. He knows I can handle myself. He shouldn't worry. I just have to figure out a plan though. I will drive myself crazy, it's like watching paint dry sitting around here," she laughed out. "Plus I need a get rich quick scheme and it's not going down out here."

"Right! I know. I want to move to like NY or something. After graduation I need to do something. My mom thinks I'm going to Princeton. I got accepted and all but I'm not even trying to go to college. I really want to act. It's been something I wanted to do for a while but you know my mom won't support that, she wants me to be like a lawyer or doctor or some shit." Simone scrunched her face up at the thought of practicing law like her mother.

"Let's move to NY," Chantel said with a new found excitement.

"What? Are you serious?" Simone asked looking at Chantel as if she lost her mind.

"Yeah. Why not? You want to act. Let's roll."

"I guess we could," Simone said after thinking about it for a few more seconds.

The last couple months of school flew by. Simone and Chantel couldn't wait for it to end so they could make their trip to NY. They didn't really have a solid plan but they knew they just wanted to leave. The day after graduation was the day.

Simone woke up to her cell phone ringing. She rolled over, grabbed it and saw that Chantel was calling.

"What do you want?" Simone asked annoyed that she was awakened.

"Bitch, get up! Start packing now, because I am half way done already," Chantel answered. She pulled the phone away from her ear to check the time, and it was 8:10 am. *Damn she is really waking me up to pack this early* Simone thought. She was planning on getting a few more hours of sleep.

"Alright damn. What time have you been up since?" Simone asked, sat up and turned her TV on.

"Since six. I told you this isn't a joke. I'm trying to be out. The truck will be at your house about 10:30. I will be following it so I'll help you pack your shit in and we're gone," she said.

"I see you got it all planned out," Simone laughed. "Alright let me get started then. I'll call you in a little while. I have to somehow finally tell my mom."

Simone still didn't tell her mom that she was wasn't going to college and that she was moving to NY instead. She just didn't think she even needed to know what she was doing with her life. She never cared any other time she thought.

"Damn, you still didn't tell her? Good luck with that," Chantel sarcastically said and they hung up.

Simone got up, took her shower and returned to her room. She slide her brown flip flops on and took a second to gather her thoughts before she went to tell her mother. Just tell her like it is, was the plan. The moment of truth she mumbled to herself and walked to her mom's office. She knocked and poked her head inside.

"Mom…" She waited for a response or acknowledgement of her presence but got none. "I'm moving to NY today," she said as she tied her towel tighter around her still wet body. Her mother just kept doing what she was doing for a minute as Simone stood at her office door waiting for a reply.

"Are you kidding me?" She finally said as she stopped and looked up from the folder she was going through.

"Yeah. Chantel and I are going. We have a place already and have been planning this for a few months now," she paused. Her mother stood still, staring at her paperwork. "I am going to pack now," she concluded.

She thought she was grown because had to handle her own issues all the time, but she didn't realize finances were a big part of her life that was supplied by her mother. She was naïve to the power and importance of money because she never had to make money on her own.

"So what about school?" she asked the obvious question.

"I'm not going. I never wanted to," Simone replied. "I am going look into becoming an actress and maybe even sing. I bet you don't even know I have a great voice," Simone said and took a step back nervous of what she might do after hearing that. She inherited her father's vocal abilities but never tried to make anything of it because she knew her mother wouldn't approve.

"Can you just think about what you're saying first? Acting and singing is neither a job nor a career! Those are one in a million careers! You can't live just thinking you want to try to be an actress with no damn experience or training. What will you do for money in the meantime? You can't live off of nothing," she said starting to get annoyed and continued to shuffle through her papers more quickly.

"Well it's already planned, so you can't change my mind. We are leaving around 11." She walked to her room and started to close the door but her mother followed and burst into the room after her.

"Child, are you stupid? You got accepted to Princeton University! You have an almost guaranteed law profession at my job when you finish undergrad and law school. Why would you throw it away on a stupid pipe dream? I am your mother and I support you, what will you do in NY without me?" She finally blew up and screamed, taking a step closer to Simone.

"Mom, I'm not going to school period. I never wanted to go. That's not even the issue anymore, and I don't need you, you haven't been there for me for anything and I do just fine!" Simone yelled back at her.

"I guess you just pay for everything then huh? That damn towel around your body is not yours!" she screamed and grabbed at the white towel. Simone clutched onto it so she didn't leave her standing there naked and embarrassed.

"This bed you sleep in, the house you live in, the clothes you wear, the sneakers and shoes! I guess you just pay for it all right?" she started screaming even louder.

They pulled back and forth on the towel while it was still on her body until her mother gripped her up by the arm. Once she did that Simone snapped and started screaming on her like she was a girl on the street. Her mother took a step back and was shocked at how angry Simone became.

"Ok," she paused and shook her head up and down. "You want to be big and tough? You think you are grown and can go move to NY on your own? With no help? Ok, go to NY and don't call me for anything. And I mean anything; I don't care what you do. So don't ask!" she said and threw Simone down onto the bed, walked back to her bedroom and slammed the door like she was an angry teenager. She poked her head back out. "You better call your good for nothing father for help, not me."

Simone sat on the bed for a few minutes trying to collect herself and calm down. All she wanted to do was leave and never come back. Her pride was going to get the best of her in the long run but at the moment Simone just thought she knew it all. She began to pack and the faster she did it the faster she thought she could get out and away from her mother. Soon Chantel and the moving trucked pulled up. Chantel's things were already packed in the truck so she got out and ran up Simone's driveway ready to help.

"You ready?" she asked with a big grin.

"Yeah," Simone said with an attitude.

"What's wrong?" she asked.

"My mom pissed me off," Simone answered and rolled her eyes. "But whatever, I'm out. Help me get my shit," she said and opened the screen door to let Chantel in. As they walked to Simone's room her mom walked out her bedroom.

"Chantel I don't know what you're doing with your life but don't bring my daughter down with you. She was supposed to be going Princeton! She can make something out of herself, and you two want to go to NY for some BS dream!" she yelled at Chantel.

"Your daughter has her own brain and I didn't..." Chantel began. Simone pulled her into her bedroom and cut her off mid sentence. She closed the door behind them.

"Please just ignore her, it's only going to be worse if you don't," Simone pleaded.

"Damn, I didn't make you do shit. You grown," Chantel argued.

"I know, just ignore her."

Simone's mother pushed the door back open, "Just get your shit and leave then. You two smart asses think you know it all." She walked back to her bedroom and turned around. "And I told Simone; don't call me for NO money. So I hope yall got a plan."

"I don't need your money," Chantel snapped back. Simone just rolled her eyes.

Her mother just laughed and went back into her bedroom. "Fast ass girls think they know everything," She mumbled to herself and slammed her door.

They packed all Simone's belongings into the moving truck and Chantel scanned for last minute things she could leave with. She decided they would need a few kitchen appliances and even though they belonged to Simone's mom, she took them anyway. They got into the car and were just about to pull off.

"Wait. I'm going to try to say bye or something at least," Simone said and looked at Chantel.

"I don't even know why, your mother is outta control," She replied.

Simone got out the car and walked slowly up the driveway contemplating what to even say to her angry mother. She tried to open the door but it was locked. She put her key in and her mother opened it from the inside before she could even turn the lock. She stood in the doorway blocking her entrance.

"What do you want?" her mother asked nastily.

"I just wanted to just...say bye." Simone said, avoiding eye contact.

"If you leave here today and you pass up your opportunity to go to Princeton, don't come back. I know you will fail, and if you leave, don't come back," her mother said with such anger.

Simone knew her mother was upset but didn't think for once that she would turn her back on her forever. Her words went in one ear and out the other. She thought she would always have a backup plan with her mother. She just had no idea of what her future held and no clue of her mother's true intentions to really cut communication after this move.

"If that's how you feel, goodbye." Simone said with a straight face even though she was hurting inside to leave on such a sour note.

She started to turn to walk away just as her mother slammed the door in her face. That relationship that was a constant friction was finally torn apart. "Bitch," she whispered under her breath and returned to the car. Off they went on their two and a half hour drive to NY.

Arriving at their new apartment was a rush of relief. The car ride was long and boring and the anticipation to start their new life in NY was eating away at them. They found the landlord, Mrs. Hattie and Chantel made the first payment. She mentioned to Simone that her brother left a little money but never said how much and offered to get them started with the first month's rent. She was really personal about her finances and Simone never pushed the issue. It wasn't any of her business anyway. Once they received their key they went up three flights of stairs to room 313. Both stood in the doorway disappointed of the dirty, grimy mess the previous tenant left. There was a main room which had pale yellowish, paint peeled walls and wooden panel floors. There was no furniture but a small silver radiator near the back window. In the kitchen there were the basic necessities, an old stove, a leaking faucet dripped into the sink and an off white refrigerator and freezer. The bedroom consisted of a window facing the side of another building and a tattered mattress that lay upon a lone steel bed frame. There were old newspapers and trash scattered randomly along the floor.

"What is this shit?" Chantel said and took the first step inside.

"Yeah really, they could have cleaned it at least," Simone said looking around at the dust covering everything including the four dirty windows in the kitchen and main room.

They walked around and went from the main room to the one bed room they would share, to the kitchen and bathroom. It was small but it was good enough for them to begin with. The driver of the truck helped them move all their belongings in and sat them in the middle of the main room floor.

"First we need to clean this place out before we unpack. We have to do that first," Simone said. She was a neat freak and the dust was just screaming for her to wipe it off. Her whole life was spent in a neatly cleaned house so this was just unacceptable.

"Well you clean and I will sleep, because a bitch is tired from driving," Chantel said and sat on the bed. The mess didn't bother her as much; she was used to living in the worst unlivable conditions.

"Um....I know you better get up. I'm not cleaning this shit by myself. C'mon we have to get cleaning supplies," Simone said.

Chantel dragged herself up out and they found the closest store and got to work. They threw out the raggedy mattress and bed and moved in their own. After hours of cleaning and unpacking they fell into their separate beds lying across the room from each other. Sore and exhausted they fell into a much needed sleep. Simone was awakened by a vigorous shaking by Chantel who was standing above her.

"Simone! Simone!" Chantel yelled in an attempt to wake her.

"What?" Simone moaned and rolled over.

"Let's go out. It's our first night in NY," Chantel suggested. "Aren't you excited?"

"Need more sleep," Simone whined.

"Come on! I want to go out. Get up!" Chantel demanded. "I'm getting in the shower, when I come out your ass better be up picking out an outfit," Chantel joked and grabbed her towel and soap, and headed into the bathroom.

Simone finally rolled out of bed and found something to wear. They got dressed and headed to a club they saw on the way to their apartment earlier. They made sure they had their fake IDs and made their way to the line.

Chantel was used to scanning her environment wherever she was. She was the one who took in all details, especially in a new place. She wanted to know what type of people where around her at all times. Once in the back of the line she noticed the group of girls in front of them. It was three of them who all looked like the just walked off the set of a rap music video. Every bit of skin they could show was showing. It didn't intimidate Chantel one bit because she knew none of them looked better than her. However, Simone saw them also and mentally doubled checked her own outfit to reassure herself.

Once inside the club, they went straight to the bar. After they gulped down their first drink, they checked out the crowd. It didn't seem to be Chantel's type of crowd.

"This is wack. Look at this- there ain't shit here," Chantel said.

Simone nodded her head in agreement and continued to look around the room, "Yeah forreal. What happened to all the hype I hear about NY ballas?"

They decided to make the best of the night so they ordered their second drink and headed to the dance floor. Simone did her own two step and frequently took a sip of her drink while Chantel gulped hers down. The mood in the club was fairly dry and the only thing that kept them interested as the small buzz they acquired from their two drinks. There were no interesting men and the only excitement was watching the three girls dressed like video vixens shake their asses on the dance floor.

"That girl got a damn eye problem. She has been staring at us since we got in here. I'm about to ask her what she want!" Chantel yelled in Simone's ear over the music.

"Who?" Simone asked looking around at the surrounding people on the floor.

"The girls that were in front of us in the line. The girl in all black," she answered.

Simone played it off, danced around in a circle around Chantel and glanced over at the girls. She was right; the girl in all black kept looking over at them. "Yeah she does have an eye problem. Maybe she's gay," Simone turned her nose up at the video vixen look alikes.

Just then a man walked in and transferred Chantel's full attention from the girls to him. She watched as he walked in and founds his friends sitting at a table on the right side of the club. It was three of them and they sat surrounding a small red table, with a bottle of Grey Goose and a pitcher of cranberry juice sitting on top. The guys sipped, laughed and just chilled, taking in the scenery.

The guy that had Chantel's focus was average height, athletic build like he may have played sports, smooth dark skin and a low hair cut. He had an immediate effect on her; something about his aura just pulled her in. She liked his sexy swag, the way he wore his clothes, his hard demeanor, everything just at perfectly on him. She knew she had to know him. She could clearly see he was fine but the question that lingered in the back of her mind was his bank account status. She didn't instantly hear the *'Cha Ching'* go off in her head when she saw him, but figured his fineness was worth finding out.

"Oh he's cute!" Simone yelled to Chantel once she realized who she was staring at.

"He sure is," Chantel answered.

She continued to sway to the music seductively as if there was a spotlight on her. Simone caught herself slightly getting jealous of the way Chantel moved her body. It was so effortless and beautiful the way she winded like an ancient voodoo call for fertility. The men around the room took notice too and Chantel got all the attention she aimed to get. Once Simone realized she was standing there looking dumbfounded over Chantel's moves, she then joined in. She surprised herself how easily she copied Chantel's dancing. It was either the few drinks or Chantel was a great person to copy off of.

Soon Chantel realized she had the attention of the guys at the table with her fine stranger and she made sure to get and keep an eye contact with him. They both locked eyes for a few seconds and she continued to keep dancing. She knew exactly what she was doing. She held up her cup and took a look inside to see it was empty.

"We need more drinks," Chantel yelled as she leaned over to Simone. "Let's go." She smirked and pulled on Simone's arm to follow her.

Chantel approached them first with a smile and leaned in over their table.

"Hey. I wanted to introduce myself. I'm new around here, and we are trying to get to know some people," she extended her hand to the fine guy first.

"Oh. I'm Trey. What's your name?" he said as he grabbed her hand.

"I'm Chantel, and this is my girl Simone," she said and motioned over to her friend. They all shook hands and introduced names. Trey was with two other guys named G and Nic.

"Yall want a drink?" Nic offered.

"You don't have to ask twice," Simone said excitedly and took a seat next to Nic. He poured her a drink and started a small conversation.

Chantel took a seat next to Trey and poured her own drink next. "So you live around this area?" she asked.

"Nah, I live in Brooklyn," he answered,

"Oh so that's probably about twenty minutes out?" she asked.

"Yeah something like that. Why you gonna come see me?" he smiled.

"No. You coming to see me," she replied and sipped her drink.

Mission accomplished she thought. She had him wrapped around her finger already. He was mesmerized by her beauty and fascinated by her confidence. The rest of the night the girls talked to the guys and Chantel and Trey and had a great connection. They exchanged numbers and finished their drinks.

"Come with me to the bathroom," Chantel yelled across the table to Simone who was twirling the straw in her empty cup.

They got up and switched away as they walked over to the bathroom. Chantel didn't even need to look back to know that Trey's eyes were glued to her ass but Simone glanced over her shoulder and confirmed it.

As they walked in the bathroom Chantel rolled her eyes to see the three video vixen look alikes in the mirror, fixing makeup and hair. Simone and Chantel slide by them and did their business as the listened to the girls have their bathroom talk.

"The tall one right?" one asked.

"Yeah him," another answered.

Then there was a silence as the girl in all black placed her pointer finger to her mouth as to say 'shhhh,' to her friends. The conversation was cut short. As Simone and Chantel came out the other girls scattered out of the way of the sinks. They all left except the girl in all black as she looked in the mirror and adjusted her breast in her shirt.

Now in the light they got a better look at the girl in all black. She was actually really pretty. She was a lighter complexion then both Simone and Chantel, with long jet black hair. She looked like she could be mixed with Asian and African American. Her face was heart shaped because of her beautiful cheek bones and jaw line. Smokey eye shadow surrounded her inviting eyes. Her body proportion was as hour glass as it gets. She had a full figured body with a tiny waist that made her curves accentuate even more. Breast overflowed out her black laced corset that squeezed in her already perfect frame and her black tights looked like they were painted on as her curves sucked in the thin, spandex material. She even had pretty toes that wore a French manicure and sat in her silver stilettos.

"I don't mean to be nosey, but I saw yall talking to them guys over at that table. Do you know them?" she looked away from her image in the mirror and asked.

"Nah just met them. Why, wassup?" Chantel spoke up first. Letting it be known she thought the girl was invading her privacy, she took a step closer to her.

"Oh I was just wondering, cause I was going to go try to talk to him but seems like yall got to him first" she said and smiled. She began to fix her hair. "I never seen yall before, do you live around here?

"We just moved on 4th street," Simone chimed in.

"Word? Well my name is Isis and if yall want I can show yall around to help you meet some new people. I'm all about having fun and making that money." she suggested and wrote her phone number on a napkin with her eyeliner.

"Aight. I'm Simone and that's Chantel. We don't really know anyone out here so that sounds cool," Simone said then glanced over at Chantel. Her facial expression said it all.

"Well hit me up next time yall trying to go out," Isis said and walked out with a smile.

Chantel snapped as soon as the girl left, "She don't seem right. What she watching us in the first place for, then going to say she about making money. What does that have to do with anything?" Chantel exclaimed.

"You're thinking too much into it," Simone laughed.

"No. you're not thinking enough. If you don't think enough someone else will and they will figure out how to think for you," she replied.

As the night came to end, the liquor was wearing off and the exhausted feeling took over. They left the club and walked down a block to find Chantel's car and saw Isis getting into her car alone. Her girls all went their separate ways to their cars the opposite direction.

"Damn!" Simone said, "Do you see her car?" They both watched as she got inside a brand new Benz. She started her car, and as she rolled down her windows, Biggie's *"One More Chance"* got louder and louder.

"Damn," Chantel said as she stuck the key into her car door. "I see I'm going to need to get me a new car," she laughed out.

6

~ Big City and Bright Lights ~

The next three weeks were full of partying, drinking, and meeting new people. They consumed their late nights at clubs and the daytime consisted of sleeping and recovering. This was an everyday routine and it was starting to take a toll on their bodies. Exhaustion was overcoming but they partied like they had no real responsibilities and in reality, they didn't. Neither one of them even looked for a job or a way to support themselves. They just enjoyed the free time and the new city. Chantel spent a lot of time with Trey, getting to know him better. She soon found out he made the type of money she was accustomed too, tax free and illegal. Simone met a guy at a club, but she didn't really like him all that much. He was just passing the time until she ran into someone more interesting. Finally Chantel realized she needed to figure out where her money was going to be coming from because she was in the mood to go shopping and didn't want to use her stash.

"We need to start looking for jobs," Chantel suggested as she devoured her fruit loops cereal.

"Yeah we do. I was thinking about going to bartender school," Simone replied, "That way, I can still be in the club," she laughed.

"I guess but don't that shit cost like six-hundred dollars?" Chantel asked.

"Yeah, something like that," she paused, "I didn't even think about that. I don't even have that to put all towards school."

"I don't know what to do. I'm really not trying to work. That's not my thing; I never worked a job a day in my life," Chantel bragged.

"Oh yeah! I got this guys card yesterday at Avalon. He said I should call him about some photo shoot or some shit." Simone said and went to her room to retrieve the card. She returned and handed it to Chantel.

"It looks cheap," Chantel said as she flipped over the flimsy card and slid it on the table.

"Well I'm going to call and see what he was talking about. Might be some easy money," Simone said and picked the card up.

"Let me call him," Chantel said and reached her hand out for the card. Simone handed it to her and took a seat at the table next to her. She finished chewing the last of her cereal, pulled out her cell phone and dialed the number.

"Hello?" the stranger on the other end asked.

"Hi. I met you at Avalon the other day, and we talked about some kind of photoshoot. I'm just giving you a call to discuss the details," Chantel said as professionally as she could.

Turns out he was a photographer named AJ, who is looking for new models to update his portfolio. He also sends his best shots to magazines like Smooth, King, Blackmen's and some other local magazines in order to get published. So he offered to shoot Simone for free and they set up a date next week. He said if the shots came out really good he could refer her to a few jobs that may pay. Simone didn't have any better plan so it sounded good to her.

"And girl, you know how most fashion people are gay. He didn't seem gay at all, he was actually kinda fine!" Simone laughed.

"Word?" Chantel asked, "you better see about that, be careful though" she laughed and rose on eyebrow at her.

That left Chantel with needing a plan of her own. Her stash of money was still thick and she wasn't worried about making money as much as Simone was yet. She knew she had a lot of time before she was down and out so she took her time on deciding what to do and figured if necessary, she could always go back to trying to play guys for their money. If push came to shove she would handle her business but Simone made it clear she didn't want her to do so.

"Why don't you just go walk around, you might meet someone or find a place hiring," Simone suggested.

"Where am I walking Simone? I'm not just going to walk around with no plan," she said back.

"Well you can't just sit around like this. Go try to get a job because sooner or later we are going to need money. Our savings won't last forever and it doesn't look like I will be America's next Top Model anytime soon." Simone complained.

"Yeah I could get a job but I'm not trying to do that shit. I can hold my own without working for now," she said and grabbed a bag of chips out the cabinet.

"What? I hope you're not thinking about getting back into your old habits. You told me over and over how you are happy to be out of that way of life. You told me how your brother got so caught up and look at where he is now. You don't want to end up like that and you sure as hell don't want to get back into playing these guys for money. You told me how stressful that became," Simone preached to her.

"Don't fucking bring up my brother, I told you about that shit," Chantel snapped back with an attitude.

Obviously still dealing with her brothers' status, she didn't want to hear anything about him, especially if he was being used as an example of what not to do. Simone had no idea of her families past struggles and didn't feel that she had the right to use her brother as a lesson.

"I'm sorry I just don't want you to think it's ok to go back to what you used to do. Get a real job and be legit," Simone said, not realizing how snobby she was being. She had no idea of what being down and out felt like. She was still under Chantel's wing, financially and emotionally. Her time would come.

For a while Chantel's main motivation for not jumping right back into her old lifestyle was for Simone. The unstable existence she once endured, she didn't want Simone to ever have to need to do it. When Simone came to visit her during the summer and she played along with her, it wasn't something she needed to do to survive, but for Chantel it was. After a few days of thinking of a plan she decided to just try to get a job. Something simple and not too time consuming just so she didn't have to deplete her funds too quickly. The stash that only her and Chris knew about was the only thing that kept her sane at night and she wasn't about to lose it. Chris put his life on the line to make that money and Chantel was treating it like it was a treasure. She decided to walk around her area and see what was hiring.

After walking a few blocks and realizing there was nothing of interest to her she decided to try to see if anything in the mall was hiring. She had to get on the subway to get there and arrived in no time. Strolling past store after store, the manikins in the window were calling her name. The job hunt was officially over and a shopping spree has just begun.

The need for new clothes overtook her since she hasn't been shopping since she was in NY and she was used to always being fresh. She went into store after store putting together outfits in her head. She fought the feeling of stealing and promised to pay for everything but her old habits were a part of who she was. She couldn't resist using her five-finger-discount. She eyed the environment, looking for security cameras and officers. She scanned for anything that would stop her from pulling off her scheme. It looked easy enough and she was a pro at it so she got to work. As she gathered her new outfits and stashed them everywhere on her she headed towards the door. She was stopped by a tap on the shoulder and she quickly turned.

"Hey! Didn't I meet you in the club?" the perky voice from behind her said.

She turned around. "Oh yeah. We did," Chantel said disappointed that it was Isis and that she stopped her mission but relieved it wasn't a security officer.

"So how have you been? Are you enjoying NY so far?" she asked and adjusted her Gucci bag on her shoulder.

"Yeah so far so good. I'm supposed to be looking for a job but found myself shopping instead," Chantel answered with a nervous giggle and looked around.

"I know how that goes; I can't stay out the mall," Isis smiled.

"Well it was nice to see you again," Chantel tried to cut her off.

"Oh yeah. Is Simone with you?" Isis asked, not ready to end the conversation.

"Nah I'm alone."

Nosey bitch she thought to herself. There was something that Chantel didn't like about Isis. She couldn't exactly place her finger on it but it bothered her every time she came across her so far.

Unfortunately Isis followed her out the store and offered a ride home. She wanted to say no, but the faster she could get her stolen goods home, the happier she would be.

"You didn't have to do that," Isis said as she drove Chantel home. Wendy William's voice was blaring loudly on her speakers. She reached over and turned down her radio.

"Do what?" Chantel defensively asked as she cocked her head back, ready to start an argument.

"Them clothes. I would have bought them for you, no problem," Isis responded.

"Oh no, it's' ok. I've been doing it for years," Chantel replied, realizing she was about to overreact. She ran her hands down the leather interior on the side of the door and wished it was hers.

"Just be careful, I don't want to bail your ass out of jail," She lectured with a laugh and slid a CD into her CD player.

"Yeah I'm good," Chantel forced a fake smile.

"So, how's Simone doing? Yall never called me!" She yelled over the music, then reached over and turned it down a little more.

"She's good; she's been focused on this modeling thing." She paused. "We both been just trying to get ourselves together and settled out here before we be all socializing," Chantel lied.

"Yeah I feel that," she answered, "I didn't know she was into modeling. I do that also a little"

"She just shot with some Photographer named AJ," Chantel shared.

"Word? That's my dude! I'm cool as hell with him," Isis responded excitedly, already knowing that.

"Small world." Chantel rolled her eyes.

When she pulled up in front of Chantel's apartment building she turned the music down again.

"Well when yall got time, give me a call for real. I got connections everywhere. So whatever yall want to do I can get it done. Tell Simone I know good photographers too," she said and started going in her purse. She pulled out some cash and peeled off three-hundred dolalrs and handed it to Chantel.

"What's this for?" Chantel asked confused.

"Just take it, hold you over until you get that job you was supposed to be looking for," she said and dropped it in her lap.

"Nah. I don't want your money," Chantel said handing it back but was thinking if she should just take it.

"Do you think I need it? I will just spend it on some more clothes, take it. I don't need it, that's change to me," she said and pushed Chantel's hand back over towards her.

"You sure?" Chantel asked looking at her as if she was fucking crazy.

"Yeah take it," she insisted. "So just give me a call. Does Simone still have my number?" she asked.

"I'm not sure, but I think so," Chantel answered.

"Well, take it again," she said. Chantel put her number in her cell phone, told her thanks, and got out still confused on why she would just hand out money like that.

All kinds of thoughts ran through her head and the main one was that she is a lesbian. There was no other explanation for her kindness to strangers and Chantel knew she had the face and body to attract men and women. When she told Simone what happened, all she could think of was that maybe she just wanted friends. Chantel reminded her she was at the club with friends and everything seemed fine. The naïve nature of Simone was starting to annoy Chantel. How could she be as blind to something obviously going on with this Isis girl? She chalked it up to her being raised in the suburbs. Everyone was out to benefit for themselves and Isis had the same mechanics working in her brain as Chantel. That's how Chantel knew Isis had a motive or an agenda. Chantel could see right through her but Simone was falling for it.

Later that day

Isis parallel parked her car and walked up two blocks. The door was unlocked so she let herself in. She walked in and saw him lying on his side with his camera pointed up at a short, brown skin model who wore black tights and a fitted off the shoulder white shirt. Trying to capture the perfect image he tried to get lower but it wasn't possible. The model saw Isis walk in and now she performed for the audience. She arched her back even further to showcase her curves even more. She used her hand to fling her hair back over her shoulders and out her face and seductively stared down at the camera.

"Baby, I'm behind you," Isis said as she took a seat at the wooden table that lay in the middle of his studio and began looking at the images on his Apple lap top.

He turned his head to see her. "Ok. I'm almost done," he replied and refocused back on his model.

Isis sat for a few minutes looking at the pictures of the last girl he shot. She wore a gold bikini and red pumps. Her body was vicious and she knew immediately she would be making good money soon.

"Hey," he said as he walked over and kissed Isis on the lips. The model gathered her bag and headed to the bathroom to change. She was glad the long shoot was finally over.

"Working hard?" Isis asked.

"Hardly working," he laughed.

"She was cute. I didn't like her outfit though," Isis spoke of the model.

"Yeah I don't know where she got the idea, but she is paying so I wasn't going to turn her away," he said with a smile.

The girl returned from the bathroom and he walked over to her. She handed him some money and he promised to have her CD in the mail by tomorrow morning. She left a satisfied customer.

"Ok cool. I will look out for it. Thanks again AJ," she said as she walked out the door.

Isis continued to go through his lap top, found the folder titled Simone and double clicked it. Over 200 images of the high yellow beauty flooded the screen. She wore a pair of light blue jeans with black pumps and a fitted black top. It definitely showed her curvy figure but the shots weren't any good. They lacked any experience and you could tell she didn't know where she wanted to go with the modeling. The images she took were in between casual and sexy but they didn't have a place in any industry, whether it was urban or commercial.

"Ah you shot my protégé I see?" Isis said as she scrolled down the page with a grin.

"Yeah she was really easy to work with, the camera loves her. She's gorgeous."

"Yeah well we need to take some of those clothes off her," Isis laughed, "Get something that will get hits on the site."

Isis badly wanted to bring Simone on her team. She knew she could make some good money from her looks and she knew she could have full control. There was a beautiful innocence that Simone possessed almost like the girl next door image. Isis was feeding off it and was already making plans for her.

"I know we can get her on our site. Throw her a couple dollars and she will think it's worth it," Isis said as she continued to inspect her images.

"Oh yeah, I think so too," AJ said, "Big money."

7

~ Pretty Girls in the VIP ~

"Simone, hurry up in the damn shower! You always take forever, I still gotta shower too!" Chantel yelled as she banged on the door.

She sat back on her bed and waited impatiently. Her cell phone started ringing and it was her mom. She imagined her mother must really be bored lately because she was calling more than usual. They didn't even talk this much when they were living together, but with nothing else to do in the suburbs, Ms. Hayes didn't really have a life.

"Hello?" Chantel answered.

"Chantel, what you doing?"

"About to get dressed, I'm going to a club," she responded.

"What are you still clubbing for? Don't you got a man now! You're going to lose him, keep shakin' your ass on every other man," she lectured to her daughter.

It was unbelievable to Chantel that her mom was telling her about keeping a man. She had so many different men in her life that she had no room to speak on it. She was in no position to try to be a role model mother and give advice.

"Mom, it's just a club, and I know how to keep my man thank you very much. Trey is meeting us there anyway," Chantel said with an attitude. "I know you didn't call me to tell me how to keep a man, what you want?" she questioned.

"I know. Well...I just wanted you to know I'm going back to Cali," she said hesitantly.

"WHAT! Why? Mom, all your going to do is get back on them drugs out there!" Chantel yelled in the phone. Simone finally came out the shower with her towel wrapped around her.

"Look, I am grown and I made my mind up and don't forget I'm the parent here," Ms. Wilson snapped back. "I am moving in with Don."

Chantel sucked her teeth, "Don? When did you guys start talking again? Is Don still using?"

"I don't know! I don't think so. That's not the point."

"How can you not care? If he is still on it, then you're definitely going to be right back at it! Stop acting like you're so damn naive to the power of these drugs. You were caught up before and it wasn't that hard to get that way was it?" Chantel screamed into the phone at her mother. She was starting to get upset.

"Look I don't need your approval. I'm the mom here. I'm going. Probably in a month or two. I'll talk to you later," her mother said and hung up.

Chantel threw the phone on the bed, went in the bathroom and slammed the door. She got in the shower and tried to relax and get her mind off her mom. She was tired of trying to look out for her mom when she never looked out for herself! I'm tired of having to be the one to deal with her she fumed in her head. Fuck that, she can go move back and do whatever the hell she wants. I'm done she finally concluded. As soon as she stepped out the bathroom Simone handed her a shot glass of Vodka.

"I saw you were a little stressed. Take some shots to get it off your mind," she said standing there with the shot in her hand and a grin on her face. Chantel grabbed the shot; they tapped glasses and took it together.

"I need a few more of them things. My mom is talking about she is definitely going back to Cali. She is about to ruin her life....again!" Chantel complained and started getting dressed.

They both took 4 more shots and were ready to go. They decided to take a cab since they were drinking and once they got there the line was winding down the block. They walked past the line to the end but didn't plan on staying there long. Chantel tried to get the attention of the bouncer, and once he looked back at her she stared deep into his eyes. He couldn't help but lust of over beauty. He leaned over to get a better look and waved them up front.

"Yall are too beautiful to wait in line," the big bouncer said and winked his eye at Simone. I guess he favored light skin over caramel because he was staring Simone all down when Chantel was the one who made the eye contact in the first place.

"Thank you. You gonna let us in then?" Simone asked flirtatiously.

"Yeah go right in, just make sure you have fun in there and shake them asses," he said and grabbed a handful of Simone's ass. She turned around and shot him an evil look.

"Come on don't worry about that, we got in for free," Chantel said and pulled her through the door.

It was crowded in the club but somehow the first person they saw was Isis. It almost seemed like this girl was stalking them. They just keep running into her and she saw them as soon as they saw her. She was with another girl who didn't share the benefit of beauty as they all did. She was short and stubby; the sort of thick that was borderline fat if she ate just another cheeseburger. Her weave looked like it needed to be redone and she had too much makeup on. She looked like she just came off from the streets, nothing classy about her. Her look was just deplorable and being surrounded by all beautiful women made it even worse.

"Hey yall!" Isis greeted the girls both with hugs.

"Hey," they replied and hugged her back. Chantel was being fake only because she was a little drunk. She rolled her eyes and searched the room to find Trey but there was no sign of him yet.

"Let me know if you see Trey," Chantel yelled over to Simone.

"Who is Trey?" Isis asked being nosey.

"He's my boyfriend. Remember the guy at the table that I was talking to when we first met?" Chantel asked proudly.

"Oh! That's what's good. Quick though," Isis laughed. "Well Simone need to hop on one of these money making machines. It's some ballers in here. Some NBA players having a birthday party up in VIP. So you know its money up in there!" she shouted and playfully nudged Simone.

"Word?" Simone said.

Chantel laughed at how similar Isis sounded to herself just last year. Although she lived most of her life that way she strongly wanted out of that lifestyle. She wanted to make her own money now and not have to depend on others. That has always been her ultimate goal.

"Let's go get some drinks ladies!" Isis shouted and grabbed Simone by the arm and pulled her towards the bar.

Already fully intoxicated Simone and Chantel followed, along with the other girl they still haven't formally met. At the bar they all

ordered Long Island Ice Tea's and Isis pulled out her wallet and paid
the bartender for all of them.

"Thanks," Simone spoke up after her first sip.

"No problem. Drink up, lets enjoy the night." Isis smiled back at
her.

They made their way through the hot sweaty bodies onto the
dance floor. They drank, laughed and danced. Immediately men
surrounded them, craving to rub their body parts on them. It didn't
take long for them to begin to grab on to their hips and grind into
them. The liquor was in full effect and they held on to their drinks and
just danced without a care in the world.

"What's your name?" the man dancing behind Chantel asked.

She ignored him at first, not wanting to talk or get to know
anyone. Her body and soul was fully happy with Trey at the moment.
She just wanted to dance. He ran his hands down her thigh and back
up near her crotch. She reached down and pulled his hands off her
thighs but continued to dance.

"I asked your name shawty," he repeated a little louder and closer
to her ear.

"It's Chantel, but I got a man," she responded without even
looking back.

"What that got to do with me. I'm just trying to be your friend.
You fly as hell," he said and ran his hands over her body some more,
getting all the free feels he could get.

"Look I got a man," she snapped.

"Where he at then?" the man said with an attitude.

Out of nowhere, Trey emerged and punched the guy in the face,
sending him staggering back. The commotion knocked Chantel's
drink out her hand and she stepped back out the way to avoid being in
the middle of it. She watched in horror as they went back and forth
throwing punches. Trey was winning and the guy was losing his
balance and hardly even defending himself anymore.

They now had the open floor because everyone backed out their
way. A guy to the right of her, who she assumed was the boy's
friend, picked up a chair and lifted it above his head ready to throw it
at Trey. Chantel reacted out of pure passion for her man and the
liquor took over her sense of reality. She grabbed a beer bottle on the
table next to her and smashed it with all her force on his head. He
stumbled back and dropped the chair. The bouncers finally got a hold
of both Trey and the guy he was fighting and pushed them towards

the door. Chantel frantically tried to keep Trey in her vision and followed behind the bouncers.

When she got outside the club she found Trey and tried to calm him down. He was still excited from the fight and didn't know where the guy was so he also had his guard up. The bouncers held the guy he fought inside the door of the club in order to avoid round two. They said he could leave once Trey left the front area.

"What was you doing letting him feel all on you like that!" Trey shouted at Chantel.

"I didn't let him. We were just dancing baby!" she defended herself.

The guy that Chantel smashed a bottle on was heading to his car. He wasn't going to let them get away with gashing his head. His pride and respect was taken and people like him couldn't handle that. Chantel spotted him walking into the parking deck holding his head and angrily talking to himself.

"Baby we gotta get out of here. That's the guy I busted the bottle on. I hope his punk ass isn't going to get a gun," Chantel warned.

"Fuck him. I got mine," Trey yelled back.

"How you get that in the club?" Chantel asked surprised, "You know what. It don't even matter, let's roll."

They walked around the block to his car and Chantel realized that she wasn't with Simone. The liquor made her forget her friend. She pulled out her cell to call her but kept getting a voicemail.

"Damn. She's not answering. What the fuck is she doing?" Chantel asked herself. She decided to try Isis. Even though she didn't like her she had no other option but to call her or go back in the club and risk being shot.

"Hey. It's Chantel. Are you with Simone?" Chantel asked as soon as she answered.

"Nah I can't find her," Isis replied, "But I'm looking for her."

"I'm about to leave with Trey, Yall should get up out of there ASAP because I seen the guy going back to his car. He might be coming back to start some shit."

"Yeah I'll find her and I'll bring her home. She'll be ok," Isis assured, with her mind already working on schemes as she talked. With Chantel out the picture, she knew she could fully handle Simone. One is easier than two she thought.

"Ok tell her to call me when she gets home," Chantel stupidly trusted Isis on account of the liquor affecting her reality.

Chantel finally leaned back in the passenger side of Trey's car, letting the breeze blow across her face. This was the first time she sat still since she started drinking, and the liquor got stronger and stronger in her system as every second passed, prompting her to close her eyes and enjoy the feeling. She was awakened by Trey picking her up out the car. She opened her eyes to stare up at his perfectly sculpted chocolate complexion face and his pearly white teeth shining under his smile.

"You a drunk," he laughed. She giggled and enjoyed the warmth of his body against hers. She felt completely protected in his strong arms and she let her body relax.

When he took her inside he laid her on the bed and she rolled over, almost immediately falling asleep. Trey pulled her pumps off, and undressed her, leaving her in her bra and panties. He undressed himself and slide in bed next to her. Her skin felt like silk on his and he pulled her close. He laid there admiring her beauty, the red laced bra that hugged her breast, and the matching thong that got lost in the middle of her cheeks. Eventually falling asleep in each others arms, Chantel missed the call from Simone.

Back at the club, Isis went to the bathroom and searched around for Simone in there. She walked past the sinks and peeked under all the stalls for feet. She wasn't sure what kind of shoes she had on but she did have a dress on so she could rule out girls with pants on. The last stall was no pants, high yellow legs inside a pretty red pump.

"Simone?" she knocked on the blue stall door.

"Yeah," she answered.

"It's Isis. You ok?"

"Come in," she slurred. Isis reached to open the door but it was locked.

"Sweetie you have to unlock the door first," she laughed at her.

Simone unlocked and pulled the door open. Simone stood there looking so worn out; she wondered if she had been throwing up.

"You ok?" she asked again after seeing her.

"I feel sick. I need to throw up but it's not coming out," she whined and leaned over the toilet.

"Awe the little baby drank too much," Isis teased, "Let's go. I will take you home. Chantel said she was leaving with Trey, so you're coming with me."

She helped her out the bathroom stall and went to go find her ugly friend that she came with. She didn't see her near the bar or on the dance floor so she called her. Since the fight, the dance floor filled back up and people resumed partying. She could hardly hear through all the music but somehow her girl had made it in VIP with the NBA players. Isis knew it was no time to take Simone home; she had a mission to accomplish and was on it immediately. She turned to Simone, and fixed her hair for her and gave her a lip gloss tube to apply to her lips. She held Simone's hand and walked to the VIP rope and waited for her friend.

"You on the list?" the big sweaty bouncer asked as he held up his clip board.

"I don't know. My girl is in there and I drove with her so I was trying to find out how I could get in," Isis responded.

Her ugly friend emerged from the crowd with a big smile and waved her up. The bouncer saw her friend and shrugged his shoulders.

"Two beautiful girls won't hurt," he said with a smile.

They both thanked him and pranced into VIP. Isis scanned her environment and instantly found money. She saw one of the starters for Knicks and made her way over to the table. He was surrounded by girls throwing themselves all over him, and his boys and teammates popping bottles, pouring drinks and singing along to the songs that beat out the speakers. She needed a way to get close to him or at least on his teammates so she decided to just go for it. She leaned over the table, letting her breast hang out her shirt and asked him for a drink.

"Yeah, help ya self," he responded pointing to the bottle on the table. "We got everything and if we don't, we order it." He took a gulp of his drink.

She Poured some vodka and cranberry juice into an empty cup and took a sip. He stared at her for a moment trying to figure out if he knew her but realized she was a stranger. His vision was a little blurry from the drinks but he knew she was fine.

"Someone invited you?" he pulled her back over and yelled in her ear.

"Nah, I just saw that this was where the real party was, so I joined," she replied with a sly smile.

"Yeah we know how to party. Come sit next to me," he motioned for his boy to move over.

She sat next to him and saw all the evil snarls she got from the girls around but ignored them. They didn't mean anything if she was sitting next to him and they weren't. She knew once she had a man's attention, nothing was going to distract it.

"So what you getting into when this is over?" she asked.

"I don't know yet," he checked his cell phone and saw there was only a remaining twenty minutes left in the club. "What are you doing?" he asked.

"Well I was hoping you didn't have plans because I got a plan for you," she offered.

"Yeah and what's that?" he asked but already knew what she had in mind. He was used to girls throwing themselves at him.

"Well my girl over here wants to fuck you," she said boldly and pointed to her ugly friend. His eyes widened and he turned to look at her ugly friend. His eyes went from her body to her face and back to Isis.

"I'm not trying to hear that, I want you," he said and ran his hand on her leg. She grabbed his hand and held it.

"Nah baby. Look I got a better deal for you then. How about my girl over here? She's cuter." She pointed to Simone who was in her own world dancing with one of his teammates.

"Yeah she is. That works for me," he said. "How come you passing your girls off?" he questioned.

"I'm not passing them off. Ain't nothing for free," she hesitated to check his reaction. He gave none; he was processing what she just said.

"You could have us both for just a G," she said as she ran her hand up his thigh.

"Oh it's like that?" He leaned back.

"Yeah, both of us," she said as she started into his eyes nonverbally promising him the best night of his life.

He paused to think about it, getting hornier by the minute. He knew he could have any woman in the club but Isis was by far the prettiest. With a combination of her and Simone he couldn't wait. The thrill of paying for them made it even more exciting and exoit for him.

"Alright, let's go."

They left in his black Escalade, dropped the ugly girlfriend off, and headed to a hotel room. He didn't want the girls to know where he lived, in case they ended up being stalkers. He had his fair share of groupies and knew the rules. In the room Isis got right down to business. She got the cash and stashed it in her purse without Simone even seeing it.

"This hotel is nice as hell, let's get in the hot tub," Simone squealed once she walked around and gave herself a tour.

"Yeah can we?" she asked the ball player.

"Yeah go ahead, I'm about to make a phone call, I will be in there in like five minutes," he answered and stepped in the hallway to call his girlfriend and make up a lie about why he would be home late.

Isis turned the water on warm and poured some bubble soap in that had a vanilla aroma. The smell filled the room and Isis began to pull her clothes off. Simone stood there realizing if they get in the hot tube they would have to be naked since no one had swimsuits.

"What's wrong?" Isis asked after noticing Simone wasn't undressing.

"Um...nothing," she replied.

She shook the feeling thinking she was being silly and dropped her dress to her feet and stood there in her bra and panties. She decided to just get in with them on. Isis pulled off her own bra and panties and walked up to Simone and leaned in close to her.

"Just relax. It's only us here."

Isis pulled down each of Simone's bra straps and reached around her back to unbutton it. She let it fall to the ground, exposing her perky breast. Isis stared at Simone's erect nipples and Simone stood still, not sure what to do. She wasn't into girls but there was no denying Isis' beauty and curiosity overcame. Simone let her eyes run up and down Isis body, admiring how perfect her body seemed to be.

"No one has to know."

Isis pulled down Chantel's panties, running her hands over her wide hips. She turned her attention to Simone's eyes. She stared into them and leaned in and kissed her. Simone suddenly lost all her will to stop things. She gave in and kissed her back. The ball player returned and stopped in the door way watching the girls. It didn't take him long to join.

On the way to take Simone back to her apartment there was an awkward silence. Simone was beginning to sober up and she couldn't believe what just happened. She went over the scene over and over in her head trying to figure out how that even went down. Isis parked across the street from her building.

"I know you not over there bitching," Isis said finally breaking the silence.

"No...No I'm ok," Simone said shaking her head.

Isis reached in her purse and pulled out a hundred dollar bill and handed it to Simone. "Take this."

"Why?" She took the money from Isis' hands.

"Just take it. Maybe you will feel better. I'm just looking out for you. I know you're not working yet so if you need anything just ask me."

"Oh...ok Thanks." Simone replied truly thankful for the money. She had no idea how she just got played.

8

~ Having Money isn't everything; Not having it is ~

Chantel twiddled her toes under the black silk sheets as she patiently waited for Trey to come back. She scanned her surroundings, appreciating Trey even more. He was upgrading his apartment more and more everyday and although he put a good amount of money into her and Simone's apartment, she spent most of her time at his. He took complete care of her on all levels. She didn't have to worry about working because anything she needed or wanted for that matter, she got from him. He reminded her of her brother, in the way that he took care of her and always put her first. The feeling of safety and a calm content overcame her as she sat thinking about Trey, but as soon as that feeling came, it left. She suddenly felt sick to her stomach, flashing back to a memory of her brother. She remembered that similar feeling of safety with her brother at one point and then he was taken away from her shortly after. Trying hard to shake the feeling, she closed her eyes for a brief moment. She opened them renewed.

"Trey baby, come on!" Chantel yelled from the bedroom. She pushed a few more buttons on the remote control but still couldn't figure out how to get to the *On Demand* movie channels. She got annoyed and threw the remote down on the bed.

"I'm coming," Trey said as he walked in the bedroom bringing the sweet aroma of buttered popcorn with him.

"I can't find the movies. You got too many damn channels!" She whined and picked up the remote control again.

He put the popcorn on his end table and sat on the edge of the bed. "It's not hard at all. I know I showed you this before." He took the remote, pointed it at the 42' in. flat screen TV he bought two weeks ago and pushed the *On Demand* button. He leaned back against his headboard but didn't get completely comfortable.

"Baby lay down," Chantel said as she tugged on his arm. He hesitated then leaned down closer to her.

"I wanted to ask you something," he finally got enough courage to say.

"What's wrong?" she asked nervously.

"I was just thinking. It's been a few months and things have been really good. You're my princess baby. I just need to know that you feel the same way I do."

Her face brightened. She thought he was going to say something negative but it was the exact opposite. Her heart needed him.

"Of course I do. I am so glad we met and that things are the way they are between us. I wouldn't know what I would do without you," she responded with a kiss on the cheek.

"And that's the thing. I know I do a lot for you and I just want to know what you want to do as far as like a career or job or something," he said.

"Umm! You're a fuckin drug dealer. You're really going to question me about my career goals and shit?" She snapped back, throwing her guard up quickly.

"Here you go. Look at you. I wasn't trying to argue with you at all. I'm just telling you this. If we are going to be serious about each other and building our lives together, you are gonna have to start something that you're trying to do," he explained and then cocked his head back, as what she just spat at him just sunk in. "If you think that I'm JUST a fuckin drug dealer then why would you want to settle for just that?" he asked defensively.

She lowered her guard down a little. "I don't want to argue either, but you came at me like I wasn't doing shit but eating off you."

"Because you're not," he replied flatly. He sat up with an attitude. "I love taking care of you. That's my duty as a man and I take pride in doing that, but I want you to have for yourself. If you can't see that then maybe I was wrong about you from jump."

He started to put his black and white Jordans on when Chantel grabbed his arm.

"Where are you going?" she questioned. Her feelings were a little hurt by the way he just talked to her but she still had to make sure her man safe at all times.

"I gotta make a run," he replied.

She sat up. "A run where? It's early; its only 1pm, you have to leave already?

"Come on. You already know," he replied getting annoyed with her questions quickly. He already knew where this conversation was going.

"Trey come on. After what just happened with Mooke and them. You know you just need to stay off the streets for a little while," she said and threw her hands up. "You know you got shit going on. You don't need to be dealing with these people right now. You don't need to be out on the streets period right now."

"So, what you expect me to just hide?" he asked sarcastically.

"No but that shit just happened two days ago. Not only are his friends looking for you right now, but you don't know what type of leads the police have."

"The police don't have shit. I wasn't the one who shot him! That was Chuckie's dumb ass," he snapped back.

"Would you please just listen to me for once? You never listen to me," she yelled.

"That's because you're always yelling at me. Damn, just talk to me. Stop yelling," he pleaded.

She stared at him for a few seconds, calming herself down. "Look you just need to lay fucking low for a while that's all." She leaned back against the soft pillows and rolled her eyes.

"It isn't that simple. I can't just disappear like Casper the friendly ghost and shit. I got things to do and you know it. You want to keep gas in that car of yours? You want to keep eating? You want to lay up in this nice apartment and watch this cable TV? You want to me to take you shopping every other damn week? The latest Gucci bag, you gotta have it right?" he shot back and stood up.

Point well taken, Chantel shut up and scrolled through the available movies with a pout on her face. He picked up his keys off the end table and leaned in to kiss her but she leaned away, putting her hand up to block him. He sucked his teeth and left.

Chantel sat there thinking about what she was going to do about a job or getting some type of income. She no longer wanted to depend on Trey even though in reality she didn't have to. She knew she could always go back to robbing, and in NY there had to be way more new opportunities. The only problem is she didn't want to get back to the risky lifestyle and she knew Trey didn't want it either. He wouldn't even allow that to go down. She really had no other options though.

She didn't even posses a high school diploma. That had to be step number one she thought.

She got on her laptop and began researching how she could get her GED and where she had to go. It wasn't a job but she felt she needed to have it in order to make any other progress. She finally got the motivation she needed to get herself together. Trey's harsh but real words made her come to that realization that it's time to be a go getter and get what she never had. All the illegal money in the world couldn't buy happiness and she knew it. They would always be living on edge, nervous of what might happen at any moment. She needed to get her mind right, and her life on the right track. It was only a matter of time before Trey came to the same realization because all drug dealers do at some point at time. Some think about it just in time to pull out of the game or some don't ever think about it until it's too late. She hoped that her inspiration and steps towards a more positive life would help Trey make the same.

Starting next week she was enrolled in classes to get her GED. She kept it to herself because she wanted to surprise Trey and Simone once she finished. Excitedly everyday from 6 to 8pm she attended class and did the best she could. Her grades were good and her teacher was impressed with her punctual attendance and genuine interest in learning. He told her to make sure that before the last day of classes to see him for a recommendation letter and that he would be of some assistance in her search for a job. Finally Simone was feeling good about herself. School was never anything of importance to her and this was the first time ever that she was really focused on it. The path to success was slowly being built in her mind, week after week as she completed classes.

Both Chantel and Simone kept pretty busy with their separate lives and didn't see much of each other like they used to. Simone was busy doing photo shoots with AJ and Isis. She wasn't making any money but she thought she had a future in it in glamour modeling. Easily influenced by Isis and AJ, her mind was set on being the next big thing in the urban modeling world. The path was clear in her mind and she patiently waited until she could start making some real money and booking jobs. Chantel was busy with her classes and spending time with Trey. Their friendship wasn't what it used to be but they still loved each other like sisters and would be there no matter what.

Over at AJ's studio

Isis sat tapping her foot and nodding her head to the beat. The music was blasting out AJ's tiny stereo that served as entertainment and a tool to loosen the models up during shoots. She pulled over his laptop and opened the internet explorer window. Rolling the mouse over to the favorite's folder, she double clicked the first website listed. She looked up to make sure Simone didn't arrive yet and continued to view the website.

"What time is she coming?" AJ asked as he looked up from his camera that he was messing with the settings on.

"She should be here any minute," Isis responded.

"I'm here!" Simone interjected as she walked in the door, mid conversation about her.

Isis quickly closed the site and hopped up and gave her friend a hug. "Hey, hun!" She kissed her on one cheek. Simone returned it.

"Hey, AJ. You ready to make magic again?" Simone asked with a grin.

"You know it," he laughed.

The shoot lasted about four hours, with two bikinis and two lingerie pieces. Somehow Simone was convinced to take more and more clothes off over the course of the last few weeks. She never did nude but close to it. It started when AJ promised her that he would try to get these pictures in this local magazine that he worked with. Within days he called her to confirm that they would be in next month's issue and he wanted to take her out to a congratulations dinner.

"So your first spread. How does it feel?" he asked with a smile.

"It's all good. It would be better if it was paying but I know, you said baby steps," she replied.

She wondered if AJ had a thing for her because she had a thing for him. She could feel herself blush more and more around him. The only problem was she wasn't sure of the kind of relationship he had with Isis. If they were just friends or more, she couldn't tell. So she decided to just keep it a friendship until she knew more.

The waiter returned, handed Simone a *Sex on the Beach* and AJ a *Long Island Ice Tea.* She shifted her weight on her other leg as she crossed them and took a sip of her drink. They exchanged playful glances all night as they enjoyed their drinks and pasta dinners. He spent a good amount of time explaining to her a lot of things about the industry she was now entering and how he could help her. He told her when her portfolio was up to standard he would send her images over to a agency that he knows the owner of and see what kind of work he could start getting her. He promised to make her a famous model and actress within the next few years. He also explained to her that in the meantime she would need to get another source of income because you could very well be struggling for a long time before your big break in this industry. He told her that he knew some avenues of income that she could look into but he would tell her about those at a later date. She ate every slice of gullible pie he served that night.

His real intentions were to get in good with her. Isis and he had a plan already in motion and were also scouting new girls to join their team. They worked a very popular high end "dating" service which really was more than dating. They shot lots of models and posted them on their site. Once they got offers from some of the most prestigious, rich, and fancy clients of theirs, they set their plan in to action. Luring the girls in with offers of cash they usually took the bait. Most of the girls had no problem accepting the easy eight-hundred dollars for a night with a rich man. What they didn't know was that Isis was taking a huge percentage, almost half but was only telling the girls she was taking ten percent. Isis was ruthless and even had some clients who weren't rich. If they girls didn't know their worth then she pretended she didn't either. Whoever was willing to put money in her pocket was all good to her.

Simone was just next on the list. Once they got her profile create, with videos and images. They knew their clients would be spending their last to have a night with her and they also knew that Simone wouldn't take long to convince. As long as they took her under their wing and made her feel like family she would listen to them and do what they suggested. All that model talk was just a cover up.

When she got home she sat watching TV when Chantel walked in.

"What's going on, bitch? I haven't seen you in like three days," Chantel jokingly asked as she closed her cell phone and shut the front door. She took a seat at the kitchen table and plopped her big purple leather purse on the floor.

"I know! Well I haven't been doing much. AJ got me a spread in Next Magazine. It's not national but it's a start. So we went out to dinner to celebrate," she grinned.

"Aww shit!" Chantel smiled back, "Wait wait wait. Is the magazine paying you?" she asked.

"No. They aren't a national magazine."

"So what! AJ and the magazine are both benefitting from using your pictures. Someone needs to come out their pockets with something. That's bullshit," Chantel snapped, "Well how was dinner at least?"

"I know, I know but I gotta start somewhere. I need the exposure and the published tear sheet. And dinner was good. I kinda like him," Simone responded with a smirk.

"Aw that's cute," Chantel cooed.

"Yeah, so we will see how that works."

"You know the rents due next week," Chantel changed the subject quickly after she realized it was Sunday already.

"Damn it is, isn't it?" Simone sat thinking.

"Yeah so I don't know what your money is looking like but I need your half. We need to go food shopping too," Chantel reminded, "Ain't shit in here to eat."

"Well I don't really have it. Can you cover it this month?" she suggested.

"I've been covering it. You're gonna need to get some type of income Simone. I can't take care of both of us forever. I'm always putting the most up for everything." Chantel rolled her eyes.

"I know. I know. I'm working on it but I just really don't have it," she whined, "I'm sorry." she picked up the remote control and started flipping channels as if that's all it would take.

Chantel sucked her teeth, got up and walked to the bedroom. She couldn't believe she expected her to cover everything again, when she's been paying it all on her own since they got in NY. If she wasn't coming out her pocket then Trey was and it was starting to get annoying. Especially since she was on the path to getting her life together she couldn't afford to take care of another grown woman. Simone was so spoiled and used to people taking care of her. She didn't realize that no one had to do that, and that it wasn't mandatory.

She didn't even want to ask Trey for the money because she was always asking him for it and it was definitely getting old. She knew she had no other choice but to ask him for it because she knew

Simone wouldn't come up with it and she wasn't about to reach in her stash to pay it all. She decided she had to say something to Simone because otherwise this would go on forever. She walked back into the living room to talk to her.

"Look I don't mind helping when you need it, but I can't do it all the time. I've been paying all the rent and pretty much supplying everything for this apartment since we've been here. I expected you to get some type of job or income by this point," Chantel said trying to be as nice as possible.

She knew what she was saying was real honest and it needed to be said but sometimes people can't handle the truth. It took all her love for Simone to calm herself down and be respectful with this conversation. The other half of her wanted to get hood on her real bad.

"Oh," Simone paused almost lost for words. "I mean I know I need to get a job. I'm sorry I didn't mean for you to pay for everything. I just don't have it," Simone sincerely apologized.

"Like I said when you need it I don't mind helping. But it doesn't seem like your even trying to help. You haven't been looking for a job even."

"I will, I promise I'm going to start looking more until I get something. I was just focused on the modeling, thinking I would be making some type of money by now." Simone shifted uncomfortably on the couch.

The air seems like it was suffocating Simone the tension was so thick. It was awkward for her to have someone tell her like it is but for Chantel it was no problem at all. Simone wasn't used to this treatment.

Simone decided she needed to get out the apartment and away from Chantel. She wanted to clear her mind and relax a little. So she called up Isis and told her to come pick her up. Isis pulled up and her car was still shiny brand new, looking lovely as always. Simone tried not to get jealous but every time she saw Isis she got envious of the things she had. Her car was so nice and she always had her hair and nails done perfectly. She even admired her style. Her outfits were always so well put together and she just looked so fresh at all times. It was like she always had money to buy the latest styles and keep her appearance up.

"So what's wrong?" Isis immediately asked once Simone got in the passenger side and closed the door.

"I need to get a job. Chantel started complaining about me not helping out with the bills and things around the apartment," Simone whined.

"Oh yeah, it's about time to get some money huh?" Isis responded. She pulled off.

"Well I can help you out in a few ways, but we'll talk about it later. Let's go get drunk!" she laughed.

"Right! I need a drink now!" Simone shouted over the music that Isis just turned up.

They arrived at a house and Isis walked right in. There were a few people walking by, headed to the kitchen for refills for their plastic cups and talking loudly over the music that blared from the owner's speakers. A few people sat around an old black fold out table playing a game of Spades. The smoke filled Simone's lungs instantly as she entered around the spades table. One girl took a pull on a blunt and tapped it in the ash tray. She held the smoke inside and her chest jumped as she inhaled it. Slowly she exhaled out the side of her mouth, handed it to the guy sitting next to her and then threw out a card. Shouts and yells exploded from each person in the game as she claimed another book and added it to her piles.

"Yeah I don't even know why yall thought you had a chance. Me and Waddie got this!" she shouted over everyone and then slapped hands with the man across from her.

Waddie shook his head in agreement, "Exactly right." He soon noticed Isis standing there watching the commotion.

"Baby girl!" he yelled towards her as he walked over with his arms outstretched, blunt still in one hand.

She leaned in and hugged him. His large muscular arms wrapped around her and one hand palmed her ass. She didn't seem to mind at all. They must have some type of a relationship Simone thought.

"Hey Waddie." She kissed him on the cheek and pulled away. She took the blunt out his hand and quickly took a pull.

"Did I say I was sharing?" he asked with a fake attitude.

"No but I didn't ask," she smartly replied and handed the blunt back. "Where are the drinks?"

"Right through there is the kitchen. Help ya self," he responded and sat back down.

"Oh yea...hey everyone this is my friend Simone," she pointed to her friend standing there like a deer caught in headlights.

Everyone rang out in unison, "what up" and returned focused back to their game. The girls headed to the kitchen and poured whatever mixture was in the pitcher into two plastic cups and began sipping. It tasted like vodka and fruit punch but a lot more vodka then punch. Simone scrunched her face up as the heat traveled down. Isis giggled at her.

"Girl, this is strong," Simone complained.

"I know it is. Just like we need it to be," she smiled and took a gulp. They walked back over to the table and watched the spade game come to an end. A token white boy walked over to Waddie and taped him on the shoulder and nodded his head.

"Come upstairs with me," Waddie said to Isis as he stood up and headed towards the steps.

Isis, Simone, Waddie, the token white boy and another short chubby boy entered an empty bed room and shut the door.

"Isis, where you been at?" Waddie asked as he sat on the edge of the bed and motioned for her to sit next to him.

"I ain't been nowhere. Where have you been?" she answered with an emphasis on you. They laughed.

"You don't come see me, don't call me, and don't ever hit me up any more," he teased.

"Well I got a new friend that's why," she pointed to Simone and smiled.

"Oh ok. I see you been busy," he nodded his head, "to busy for ya boy, it's cool. I understand." He grinned. She playful slapped his arm and laughed.

"Simone do you smoke?" Waddie asked as he tore open a fresh blunt in preparation to roll.

"Nah I don't," she responded and found her way to the last empty chair.

"She is tonight," Isis chimed in and shot Simone a cold stare.

Simone was taken aback by her response but figured it wouldn't hurt to try it. She guzzled down the rest of her drink quickly so she wouldn't be as nervous to smoke. Isis was also finishing her drink and spotted a bottle of vodka on the end table. She leaned over and grabbed it and poured herself some straight and motioned for Simone to come get some too.

"I never smoked before. I don't know if I know how," Simone whispered to Isis.

Isis smiled and took a sip of her drink. "It's easy. Just take a deep pull of it in, hold it for a second, and then exhale it out slowly. Watch me," Isis said as she took the blunt.

She licked her lips and placed it in her mouth. Inhaled deeply and held it. She blew out the smoke slowly and almost seductively and smiled.

"Your turn," she passed it to Simone.

By the end of the night, Simone was as high as a kite. She sat slumped back against the headboard of the bed and stared into the air. She looked like nothing mattered to her. The two other boys left and only Isis and Waddie remained to finish up the third blunt. Isis stood up and left the room to find the bathroom. She found it and went headfirst into the toilet and threw up. Too much to drink and smoke had her stomach flipping and her head pounding. She took a minute to look in the mirror and laughed at how low her eyes were. She cleaned herself up and went back to the bedroom. The door was closed. She turned the knob but it was locked so she banged on it.

"Simone!" Isis yelled and banged some more.

Waddie opened the door slightly and peeked out. He was holding his pants up by the belt buckle in the front. Obviously interrupted.

"What the fuck are you doing?" Isis whispered fiercely.

"You already know what it is," he responded and stepped outside the door, closing it behind him.

"You are bugging right now. That's my bitch, how you just gonna try to fuck her and be sneaky about it," Isis snapped back, being careful Simone didn't hear her.

"I wasn't trying to be sneaky," he said trying to calm her down.

"Well give me my fuckin money then," she shot back, not calming down at all.

"I was going to give it to you," he reached in his pocket and pulled out a wad of cash and handed her some. She quickly counted it and stuffed it in her purse with an attitude.

"Alright, and hurry up. I'm gonna be in the car so when you done just send her outside," she said finally calmed down since she had her cash.

She held on to the banister and made it down the steps and out to her car to

Waddie stepped back into the room, closing the door behind him. Simone lay on the bed with no clothes on under the burgundy blanket. She fell asleep that quickly, knocked out by the liquor and weed.

Immediately he pulled his pants down and stepped out of them, then pulled the condom out the pockets. As he climbed on the bed he slid his hands up her legs across her hips. Groping her ass sent a chilling feeling through his body that ended in the head in between his legs. He cupped her breast in his hands and admired what he was about to get into. She's beautiful as shit, too good to be rolling with a nut like Isis he thought. The thoughts of a good girl gone lost quickly faded out his mind as he let his eyes wander to her paradise below. Cleanly shaven and pretty as can be he couldn't wait any longer to get inside it.

He stuck his fingers in his mouth, then stuck them inside her and worked them around getting her body ready for him to enter. She was wetter then he even imagined. His mind was no longer thinking logically and before he put the condom on he put himself in her. Soft squeaks of the bed springs and his heavy breathing were all that could be heard. She squirmed a little and slowly woke up. She could tell someone was on top of her but her vision was so blurred and doubled that she didn't know who. He saw the startled look on her face and began working harder and harder. Pounding in and out of her she struggled to sit up and pull away but he was so much bigger then her. Getting a nut was all that mattered to him at this point so he laid down placing all his weigh on top of her. He worked himself in a frenzy as he finished inside of her and laid there panting, trying to catch his breath.

Simone continued to squirm underneath him and tried to yell at him to get off of her. All that came out her mouth were inaudible slurs. Finally she dug her teeth into his neck and grabbed a mouthful of flesh. The reaction could only be coined as priceless as it sent him jumping up in pain.

"Bitch, what the fuck is your problem," he yelled as he reached up and grabbed his neck. She jumped up and grabbed her clothes and quickly tried to pull her jeans on without even worrying about her panties.

"You knew what it was, why you acting like that?" he screamed at her. He moved his hand off his neck and checked his hand to see if there was blood. "Get the fuck outta my house, crazy bitch."

Silent and embarrassed she pulled her shirt on and stuffed her bra in her purse. Then grabbed her heels and stumbled towards the door.

"And tell Isis, don't bring no scary bitches like you over here again," he pushed her out the bedroom door and slammed it shut.

Trying to gain her composure she stood at the top step before attempting to go down. When she safely made it to the bottom step she sat and put her heels on. The next immediate thought was, where is Isis and how did I end up in the bed? She looked around downstairs, through the living room, past the spades table and peeked in the kitchen. Isis was nowhere to be found. She pulled out her cell phone, called her and was told to come out front.

"Girl come on," Isis said as she waved her over to the car. Simone jogged across the street and got in the passenger side.

"Why did you leave me in there with him?" Simone said immediately after she sat down and closed the door.

"I had to make a phone call. What's wrong?" she asked nonchalantly.

"All I know is that I was sleep, and next thing I know he was on top of me!" she shouted.

"Forreal?" Isis questioned excitedly, "Who was? Waddie? The one we smoked with?"

"Yeah," Simone responded shaking her head, "Did you mess with him? I thought that was your man or something."

"Oh no, we are just really good friends." She flagged that thought off knowing he was really just one of her many clients. "So did yall have sex?" She tried to sound sympathetic.

"Yeah, but I didn't want to, I woke up and he was inside me!" She shouted. The idea of being raped didn't seem to be a big deal to Isis as Simone explained the situation.

"Oh damn! My bad girl, I didn't know he was gonna do that shit," Isis lied, "You alright?" She acted like she cared.

"Yeah I guess, but I don't think he used a condom. I didn't see one." Simone sulked at the thought of contracting a STD or getting pregnant.

"Waddie's a fuckin dickhead," Isis replied. "I will get at his ass later," Isis lied again. "Let me get you home."

As she pulled up to Simone's apartment complex she reminded her to give her a call tomorrow so she could talk to her about the money making opportunities she had in mind for her.

9

~ Turned Out ~

Squinting to see in the dark was slowing down Chantel's rush to her bed. Exhausted from her surprise shopping spree with Trey, she couldn't wait to be able to close her eyes. Her hands full with bags from Macy's, Nordstrom, Bebe, Steve Madden, Tiffany's, Victoria Secrets and many more, she stumbled along trying to get to her bedroom without falling in the dark. Bypassing the light switch because her hands were full she thought her eyes would adjust to the midnight black. She was wrong. Just before she walked right into the bedroom door she protected herself with an outstretched hand. After realizing the door was closed she dropped her bags from her right hand and tried the door knob. It was locked.

Just then she thought she heard a grunt. She stood completely still to stop her bags from ruffling and leaned in close to the door. She was right. Another grunt followed by a consistent movement of the bed against the wall seeped through the door. Damn she's at it again she thought.

"Why didn't I know she was a whore before I moved in with her? A broke whore at that," she said under her breath as she made her way to the couch.

She flipped her pumps off and fell instantly asleep but was awaked in a matter of minutes by a knock on the apartment door. It took her a minute to realize what she just heard and walked over to answer it.

"Who is it?" she asked with an attitude. She leaned in close to the door.

"Isis," the voice on the other side responded.

There was a moment of hesitation before Chantel decided to let her in but she had no choice, "Hey, wassup?"

"Hey girl!" Isis leaned in, hugged Chantel and pulled away with a kiss on her cheek.

"Damn I see someone went shopping! All these bags; Tiffanys? Word?" Isis squealed as she walked in and hovered over the merchandise.

"Yeah Trey took me shopping," Chantel said as she took her seat back on the couch.

"Oh I was gonna say, girl you balling like that?"

"Hell to the no. I am not ballin…but that's part of my master plan. I will be one day," Chantel joked.

"Well that's exactly what I came over here for. I got a suggestion for you and Simone. It's a good come up, easy money. I know yall both still looking for jobs so this might hold you until you get what you really want."

Chantel was all ears. Making money was always a main objective in her mind and she defiantly wanted Simone to get on it.

"How can we make this come up?"

"Dancing." Isis replied.

"Oh. You talking about stripping? Yeah I'm not down with that. I can come up some other way. I ain't that down and out as you see by the Tiffany bags," Chantel scrunched her face up at the thought of shaking her ass for someone's dollar bill.

"It's not even that bad! You probably just scared of them bullshit horror stories. I've been doing it for a just a year now and you see what I'm pushing. I don't have any money problems ever; I'm well taken care of. For just a few hours at night, you can bring home a minimum five-hundred at my spot; that don't even include your private dances or parties. Shit you can't tell me there's something better out there," Isis tried to convince her.

"Damn five-hundred a night?" Chantel questioned.

She pictured herself in a turquoise full body thong with a Pamela Anderson, platform clear stiletto. The vision of fat, sloppy, greasy man's hand reaches up and pulls her by the hip for a personal dance.

"Nah I can't do that shit!" She quickly came to the realization.

"Suit ya self! Where Simone at?" Isis questioned.

Just then a short and stocky light skin boy opened up the bedroom door and began to walk out. Embarrassed by the women's eyes on him, he tried to hurry out.

"Excuse me, you can say hello to the people in the apartment," Chantel snapped at the boy.

"Oh my bad, ma. How y'all doin?" he responded, waved a hand, then let himself out.

Simone peeked her head out her bedroom door with a smirk, "Hey bitches!"

"Come here, hoe!" Isis joked, "Do you want to get down with this money or what?"

"Money? Did somebody say money?" Simone's face perked up even more, "Wait I need to put some clothes on."

"If you don't bring your ass out here. With my plan you're gonna be naked anyway, so you should just get used to it," Isis pointed out.

Simone wrapped her arms around her body that bore only a simple pink, cotton, bra and panty set. She rubbed her hands up and down her arms and plopped on the couch. The small hairs on her legs and arms began to rise.

"So what's this plan. I'm down," Simone stupidly accepted before knowing the offer.

"Alright, so I work at this club. I bring home like five-hundred a night. That don't even include private parties and shit." Isis tried to make it sound so sweet, knowing that it was a hole of hell in that club. The only thing that brought Isis happiness was money and bringing people into her misery with her.

The same exact reaction Chantel had, showed up on Simone's face, "Dancing?"

"Yea, you dance on stage three times a night for like fifteen minutes. Then you walk around the spot doing little lap dances. I'm telling you it's easy as hell. Dumb easy money!"

"Um I don't think I can do that," Simone hesitantly said then turned to get Chantel's reaction.

"Don't look at me. I already said I'm not down," Chantel snapped, "I got a man; he is not letting me shake my ass for no other men."

"Damn I forgot about him that quick," Isis laughed. "Well Simone you down? We can go tomorrow, I'll bring you in."

Simone sat thinking for a second. The easy money was calling her name. She could literally hear it. Dollar signs danced in her head as she imagined all the things she could buy with five-hundred a night.

"You really make five-hundred a night? Every night?" her curiosity was taking over as well.

"Just about. Some nights may be slow, but you usually have your regulars who take care of you. If you don't make enough on stage then you will make it up in dances. I do private parties but not often because a lot of the girls don't like to. So I never go alone. That's why you need to get down with me and we could both do them. Their even easier then the club. You just go drop it a few times on a group of them and that's it! You shake your ass in the club for free every damn night. You should just get some gwop for it!"

Chantel grabbed her cell phone that was vibrating and giving off a neon yellow light. Her face lit up as well when she saw the name. She took her call to the bedroom for privacy.

"I don't know. I mean it sound all good but I know it's gonna be some bullshit that come with it. I'm not trying to have no men disrespecting me," Simone returned.

"Listen you already disrespecting ya self by dancing. So you should just get over that now. You have to really look at it for what it is. You are using your body to get paid. Do what you gotta do, make the money and get the fuck out. It's simple. You can't let ya emotions or doubts get in your way because that's how you get walked all over. So suck it up, and come with me tomorrow because I'm not taking no for an answer anyway. You're broke. You ain't got shit else to do."

Simone rolled her eyes at Isis's sternness. The mere thought of stripping made her sick but she knew the money was good. How can you turn down five-hundred a night? Fuck it; all I need is a couple drinks, she thought.

"I'm in," she said solemnly. Isis shook her head up and down for approval.

5 minutes later

"What the fuck is yall doing in here?" Chantel screamed over the music blasting from the Sony stereo as she walked out her bedroom to join them.

Simone was on all fours, concentrating on making her ass cheek jump through her pink panties and Isis was leaned down coaching her.

"I'm teaching her how to booty pop!" Isis laughed.

"You two look like a ghetto hot mess right now," Chantel said and turned her nose up at her friends jokingly.

"You know you want to learn how too. Stop fronting," Isis retorted.

Chantel's face displayed a devilish grin, "You right. I always wanted to know how they do it." She ran over to join them on the floor. "But don't think you're going to have me in that club."

When they finished playing around in the living room Isis headed home. It was getting late and both the girls were exhausted from putting so much concentration on their butt cheeks. After Isis left, Chantel got in mommy mode.

"This was all fun and all but I hope you really don't go into that club with Isis. It sounds all sweet but there have got to be better ways. Believe me its sugar on the outside but its thick as hell on the inside. It's going to be a lot to deal with," Chantel warned.

"Oh I know. I just want to go make some money and be out though," Simone responded.

"I'm telling you, it's going to be more then you can handle. I still don't think that girl is up to any good. She just is so sneaky."

"You still don't like her? I thought you were over that. She is cool. I mean she is a little out there, but I don't think she's purposely trying to sabotage us in any way or be sneaky."

"Well something about her isn't right. Just don't play her to close. That's all I can say."

The next night Simone stuck by her word and went along with Isis to the club. In her gut she didn't want to because she just knew it would be difficult for her to get over her nerves. She was comfortable with her body and knew it was built better than most but what made her scared was the men that would be gawking and grabbing it. She lacked the same confidence Isis had. She was able to walk in a room and grab everyone's' attention and work it well. Simone on the other hand grabbed attention for the simple fact she was beautiful but she didn't know how to hold that attention the same way Isis could. She was used to following Chantel's lead.

Upon entering the side door that led downstairs to the dancers changing room, Isis was greeted by a man dressed in all black. He stood tall towering over the ladies, his body was clearly a mass of muscle and Simone assumed he was a bouncer. It was still early in the night so the club wasn't open for business yet but bartenders and bouncers were prepping. Isis walked over to a back office and tapped on the door.

"Come in," a husky voice yelled through the door.

Inside sat a pot belly middle aged white man behind a large metal desk covered with folders and papers. His hair was greasy and slicked back exposing his full crater face. Around his neck dangled a small silver cross. It sat on top his exposed chest that his dingy wife beater failed to cover. He looked like he was lost in a pile of work and didn't know where to even begin. He dropped the folder from his right hand when they walked in. A girl sitting next to him dressed in a pink sweat suit and a pair of white sneakers got up as they entered.

"Hey, Daddy!" Isis squealed in her usual over excited tone. It seemed like her energy was never down. No matter when, what, or where she was, it was always up.

"Hey, Marlene," she said to the girl in pink.

"Ah, Isis. My lady," he answered and stood from his seat.

She walked over and hugged him, ending with a kiss on the cheek. Simone's gut flipped a few times as she watched the exchange between them. 'Daddy' grossed her out by just the sight of him. If you look up pervert in the dictionary, you would find a picture of him.

"Hey, Ice," the girl answered, leaned over and kissed the crater face man goodbye and left the room without another word.

Simone immediately thought this man was some type of mastermind. He was the most disgusting looking guy ever but is constantly surround by the most beautiful of women. Must be nice, she thought to herself.

"I have a new dancer for you." She pointed over to Simone with a smile. "I can personally vouch for her. She's about her business, no games and won't bring you any problems."

The fat man behind the desk stepped up front to get a better look at her. He put his finger out and swirled it around as to imply for her to turn for him. She rotated around a full circle showing her shapely figure. He was impressed by her body. Secondary he loved her cute face.

"Can you dance?" he broke the silence.

"Yeah," she blushed getting nervous already.

He walked back behind his desk. "Ok, give me a few minutes and show me on the stage. Tell Chuck to give you some music." He sat back down and picked the folder back up.

Isis winked at him and walked out the office, closing the door behind her. She moved close to Simone's ear and whispered sternly, "Don't embarrass me."

Simone took the comment as a threat and her nerves took over. She smiled nervously. Here goes nothing, she thought to herself.

"Just go up there and feel the music. Ignore anyone in here and just dance. Be sexy because you are. It's natural," Isis coached her now with a little bit more encouragement.

She knew there was no turning back at this point. She looked over at the bar and yearned for a drink. Liquor was definitely needed at this point.

"Can I have a shot?" Simone asked Isis.

She shook her head yes and in that very second Simone was behind the bar pouring herself a shot of Bacardi 151. She threw it back immediately and scrunched her face up from the heat that traveled down her throat into her chest. She shook the feeling and headed to the stage just as Daddy came out the office to watch.

She wore a grey tank top and a pair of black tights with peekaboo toe black shoes. Before she emerged from the curtain she took a second to pull her game plan together. "Fuck it. Just do the damn thing," she said to herself.

Seductively walking out onto the stage, she imagined being with the sexiest man ever and what she would do to please him. Her womanly instincts took over and her hips lead the way. The smooth slick movements she made even surprised herself as she stepped outside her character. Completely turning into a sex kitten in a matter of seconds, Isis and Daddy stood impressed at her fluid maneuvers as she removed her top and bottom. Remaining in a simple black thong and a black lace bra that held her breast like hands, she ended the song.

"She's got it. She's definitely got it. Run her the rules. She's got it!" Daddy exclaimed and returned to his office. Isis smirked, happy that she pleased Daddy. She followed him into the office and closed the door before Simone got there.

"Now I better not get any problems from her. It's always the best ones that bring me bullshit to my club." He pulled open his bottom drawer and dug in, pulled out a wad of cash.

"Naw she's cool. She's pretty quiet and she's my girl so I will keep an eye on her," Isis assured. He handed over five crisp hundred dollar bills, paying her for her recruitment efforts. She worked well for daddy and whenever she was able to bring a quality girl into the club, he paid her nicely.

The next few weeks Simone was getting used to her new routine. Danced all night and slept all day. Her pockets were bigger than ever and she felt on top of the world. Every other morning returning in at around 6am, she stashed her cash away until she could take it to the bank. She upgraded her clothes, paid all her bills and partied like a rock star with Isis. Things just seemed perfect to her. The other dancers in the club paid her no attention so she didn't have any problems there. Her customers were respectful enough to not piss her off yet and she had money in the bank.

Isis decided to take it to the next level and invited Simone out to a private party. There were always parties to do and they make better money at the parties than in the club. It was simple; you dance for them all, and then work the room individually just like at the club. If there was a main man of the night you pay him special attention. Isis knew that usually at these parties more than dancing went down and was fully prepared to bring Simone into it.

"We are leaving the club after your solo dance; I got a private party for us," Isis said to Simone.

"Word? Where at?"

"It's not a bachelor party or anything. It's just a bunch of guys hanging out who want a couple dancers. So it's just me and you going. More money for us, we only have to split it two ways."

Simone plopped down in the chair in front of the vanity mirror. She turned her face right to left to check her makeup. "I don't know about going alone. We are going to be around a bunch of rowdy drunk men." She looked over at Isis.

"Girl, I know. I'm not stupid. AJ always goes to my private parties with me to watch out." She dug in her purse and pulled out a small purple pouch. She leaned on the table holding the vanity mirror and faced her. She opened the pouch and pulled out a small white pill. "Here." She handed it to Simone.

"What's that?" She scrunched her face up.

"It's an E pill. Just take it; you'll need it to get through your first party. Those dudes can get annoying."

"I don't know about that. What does it do to you?" she cautiously questioned.

"Nothing it just makes everything feel real good. Puts you on some new shit. It's like being drunk but everything you touch just makes you feel so relaxed."

"I will just take a few shots. I'm not trying to take no pill," she replied and fluffed her hair.

"I didn't ask if you wanted to take it. I said take it," Isis snapped back and put the pill on the table in front of her. She stared at her and waited for her to take it.

"I really don't want it," Simone whined.

"Take the fucking pill. You seriously need to stop with all this being a baby shit. Grow up."

Simone sucked her teeth and picked up the pill, observing it.

"Damn, you're such a bitch. I'll cut it in half," Isis snapped and went in her purse to retrieve a hidden razor blade. She sliced the pill and tucked half away back in the purple pouch. Simone picked up her half and slowly placed it on the back of her tongue and swallowed.

"Good girl. Now pack your bag so we can leave. Fuck your solo dance, we will make more money tonight at this party anyway," she demanded.

On the way out the club, the girls took a shot of Vodka and headed to the car. It was clear that Simone was starting to feel the effects of the drugs and the liquor. Her mind was at ease and her body soon followed. She slumped back in the passenger side and let the breeze from the window whip across her face. Any worry or cautious thoughts soon left her mind. Isis pulled in a parking spot then called AJ. He was around the corner on his way and would meet her inside.

The music could be heard from outside the door as Isis and Simone carried their duffle bags towards it. Simone sang along to her favorite rappers song, 'ok start with straight shots and then pop bottles, pour it on the models, shut up bitch swallow.' She bounced to the beat as Isis banged on the door. A tall skinny boy answered the door with a grin on his face. He waved them in and Isis told him they needed to change. She spotted a bottle of Grey Goose on the table and grabbed it as they went into the bedroom.

Isis slide off her grey sweat pants and pulled her red tank top off as Simone just sat on the bed watching. Isis noticed she wasn't changing and realized she must be high as hell. She walked over to the Grey Goose bottle in her bra and panties and took a gulp. Letting the burn slither down her chest, she plopped down next to Simone and handed her the bottle. A huge smirk came across her face as she took the bottle and gulped down a mouthful. Isis leaned over and snuggled her face close to Simone and kissed her on the neck.

"Come on. You gotta change," Isis said as she ran her hand down Simone's thigh. A knock on the door interrupted them.

"We not finished changing," she shouted out through the closed door.

"It's AJ. I'm just letting you know I'm here."

"Ok," she responded and put the rest of her bikini on.

When both were done they left the room and entered into a world of hungry beast. All sitting around drinking, smoking, eating and patiently waiting, their excitement level peaked as the two beautiful redbones walked out the bedroom. AJ stood in the back corner and held up a video camera taping the episode and no one even noticed or seemed to care. He handed a CD to the guy sitting next to the CD player. Isis took the lead as expected and as soon as the beat dropped she dropped in the middle of the floor in a split. Simone let her do her show and slowly walked around the room, allowing everyone to admire but not touch her body. She teased them all as Isis performed. The men got more and more rowdy with anticipation to get their hands on the women.

Once Isis was finishing up in the middle of the room, she switched roles with Simone. Isis took her turn around the room giving lap dances and collecting her tips. Simone didn't spend as much time in the middle of the room once she saw the tips. She got up and started working the room as well. After getting a reasonable amount of money, Isis looked over at AJ who was speaking to a group of three of the men. She winked at him and grabbed Simone's hand. She pulled a chair to the middle of the floor and sat Simone on it. Her seduction skills came into play as she playful kissed down her neckline down to her breast. The men loved it and threw more and more dollars. The kisses went lower and lower down her breast, to her stomach, around her thighs and then to her love spot. Simone didn't even think twice about allowing it, her mind was lost in a lust she never knew existed. Although this kind of thing happened before, it was more personal, just between them two and a ball player. She didn't let her mind think about it and just went with what felt good, and that was Isis between her legs.

"Take Simone in the room," AJ said as he tapped Isis on the shoulder.

She stood up and he handed her the camera. They went into the bedroom followed by one of the men in the room. Isis sat the camera on the dresser in front of the bed and joined the two on the bed. She reached over and caressed Simone's face and watched her eyes roll back in her head from the simplest touch to her cheek. She knew that E pill had taken her over. She reached down and pulled her bikini bottom off and ran her fingers in her wetness. Simone groaned wildly and as she gripped the sheets. Isis then began to unbuckle the guy's pants and pulled them off. They both shared the growing mandingo in their mouths as the video camera rolled.

10

~ Friend or Foe ~

"Trey, baby hurry up," Chantel whined as she fixed last minute touches on her makeup, "We have reservations, we need to be there."

"I'm coming. If you would have let me know about my surprise dinner in a more advanced time then there would be no rushing," he laughed.

"Shut up!" she playfully shouted back into the bedroom.

"See you're fuckin up."

He entered the living room looking drastically different than he ever does. He had on dark denim jeans, black hard bottoms, and a white button up on. Usually you wouldn't catch Trey in hard bottoms but Chantel insisted that he dress up for their dinner date tonight.

"I'm ready."

"Good, lets' go." She grabbed his hand and they headed out.

They pulled up to TAO Restaurant and their growling stomachs quickly led them inside. Upon entering there was a huge Buddha statue that was impossible to ignore. The ambiance was upscale and city chic.

"Do you have something to say?" Trey questioned, wondering why Chantel was staring at him from across the table.

"Nope," she smirked.

"Come on, something has to be on your mind. Why did you decide to want to go out to dinner tonight randomly? Then you're sitting across from me looking all sneaky."

"I'm not sneaky! I just wanted to go out tonight. That's it," she replied and eyed the menu.

"Yeah I don't believe you." He sat his menu down and grabbed hers. "What's going on love?"

"Ok fine! Damn baby, beat it out of me."

A slender woman came over with her notepad. "Good evening. I'm Julia and I will be your server tonight. Can I start you off with drinks?"

"Ice tea. Sweetened," Chantel said.

"A Sprite," Trey said. She walked away and he turned his attention back to his girlfriend. "So, what's up baby girl?"

"Well it's nothing major, but I just wanted to tell you I finished my GED and I'm actually enrolled in community college for the fall semester." Her face glowed with pride.

His head cocked to the side, "Baby girl!" he exclaimed. "That's wassup! I had no idea you were even working on that."

"Yup," she replied still smiling from ear to ear.

"Aww look at my baby trying to get all smart and responsible and shit. Let me find out," he cooed at his girl.

"Shut up. I'm not trying to get smart, I'm already smart!" she shot back and laughed.

Chantel's cell phone began to vibrate on the table. She flipped it over and saw it was her mother. "Hello Mother," she instantly said as she put the phone to her ear.

"Chantel, what you doin?" she questioned.

"I'm at dinner with Trey, what you want?" she asked, getting annoyed already.

"I just was checking on you but you're busy. Call me when you leave," she sounded disappointed.

"You sure? You never call to just check on me. What you want?" Chantel smelled a lie.

"Damn never mind I don't want to check on you then. Bye!" She hung up.

The look on Chantel's face gave her confusion away. "Something's up with my mom. She's being funny."

"Yeah. What's wrong?" Trey asked.

"I have no idea."

"Baby, look to your right. Isn't that your friend?" he interrupted and nodded his head to his left.

Chantel slowly turned and looked over to the other side of the restaurant. She saw a middle aged grey haired white man in a black suit. He leaned over across the table and used a napkin to wipe the young woman's lip clean of some red pasta sauce. She smiled and licked her lips to make sure it was all gone. The man sat back down comfortably in his chair and took a sip of his wine.

"That's that hoe Isis." She turned back to Trey and they both stared at each other. "You already know I have to go over there and be nosey," she grinned.

"See I knew I shouldn't have said anything. Sit your nosey ass down and mind your own," he laughed.

"You know you want to know why she's at dinner with that old man too!"

"Don't start no drama, come on ignore it," Trey pleaded.

"Nope. You know I don't give a shit about drama. Be back." She stood up, fixed her dress and flirtatiously blew a kiss at Trey as she walked across the room.

As she approached the table, Isis fixed her face from shocked to a fake happy to see her. She didn't expect to see her at all and it caught her off guard.

"Hey Isis. I was just having dinner with Trey when I saw you over here. How are you?" Chantel played her fake friend role and leaned in and gave her a kiss on the cheek.

"Hey Girl. I'm doing good. Oh and this is Frank."

They greeted each other and Chantel was off back to her table. Satisfied with what she found out she plopped down in her chair across from Trey.

"He's married. I saw his ring," she informed him.

"Damn. I wonder what that is about," he shook his head.

"Who knows? That girl is sneaky as hell. She is always involved in something. He's probably paying for that ass."

After dinner and a few drinks it was still early. They drove through the city streets unsure of where to go next. They discussed their options and going home to bed at this hour was defiantly out.

"Let just go to a club, get a few more drinks and wrap this up in your bed," she grinned.

"Let's do a strip club. I've never been to one with you." He looked over to see her reaction.

"Cool, I'm down."

The DJ in the club was blasting Uncle Luke, like they were somewhere down in Miami. It set the mood just right. The girl on stage was a thick Buffie The Body type dancer doing tricks to the beat with her cheeks. They took a seat near the right end of the stage and a busty woman came over and took their drink orders. Chantel was already feeling a little buzz so she stood up and danced in front of Trey like she was one of the dancers. He pulled her down into his lap and planted a kiss on her lips. She rolled off him and back into her seat and bounced to the beat. The waitress returned with their drinks and a stack of singles that he requested for a hundred dollar bill.

He handed her a stack of singles and her face lit up with excitement. "Ha I'm going to make it rain baby!" She squealed. He just laughed at her. For Trey, being in the strip club was so normal. He was in one every few days at the least. Chantel hasn't been to many so when she does go she wants to turn into a man. Throwing dollars and treat the dancers like they were less than her. She respected their hustle but wouldn't be caught dead doing it so she had fun with it.

Trey looked around the room at all the dancers on the floor. He wanted to buy Chantel a lap dance. He was curious to see how she would react to it. He let her down her drink first.

"Babe. Find the best dancer on the floor," he leaned over to her ear to yell over the music.

She scanned the room of dancers and no one seemed to catch her eye. She looked up on the stage and saw a dancer sliding from the top on the pole so fast it looked like she was going to slam into the floor. Instead she ended at the bottom in a split and twirled her legs back up the pole. She put her hands on the stage and let her legs off the pole and ended on her back. Chantel was in amazement so she stood up and started throwing her singles. "Go head girl!" She shouted and continued to throw her money.

Trey pulled her down by the hip before she threw all her singles to her. "I guess you found who you like?" He smiled. He waved the girl over once she got off the stage and paid her for a dance for Chantel. She walked over to Chantel, took her drink out her hand and placed it on the table in front of her. She put one knee between Chantel's legs and leaned forward placing her breast in her face and she winded to the beat. You could see Chantel was uncomfortable but a good sport about it. She let the dancer do her thing and gave her a few dollars in her thong and sent her on her way.

"You liked it?' he asked hoping she did.

"It was weird," she giggled.

"Babe I want to fuck you right now. Let's go," he said not holding anything back.

"Let's roll," she said with a smirk, "Let me use the bathroom first."

She finished up her last drink and walked wobbly over to the bathroom in the hallway near the entrance. Trey picked up his phone to answer it and watched the girl on the stage do her thing. He hung his phone up after a quick conversation and finished up his drink. He looked over to his right and saw a familiar face walking out from downstairs. Simone. She walked through the guys until she noticed Trey waving her over. Her face brightened as she ran over and gave him a hug.

"Hey Trey," she said as she pulled away. She let her hands run down his arms and for the first time realized how muscular they were. Nice, she thought.

"What's good girl? I didn't know you were a dancer," he said surprised.

"Yeah I started like a month ago. Gotta make that money." She looked around realizing Chantel wasn't there.

"Where is your girl at?" she asked curiously. She ran her hands up her chest and fixed her bikini top.

"She's in the bathroom." He couldn't help but admire her body. It was smack in his face and her body was surely nothing you could ignore.

She leaned down to whisper in his ear, "If Chantel wasn't here I would give you a dance."

He laughed nervously and shifted in his chair, not knowing how to respond to her comment he said nothing.

"Think about it, maybe another time," she smiled and turned to walk away, "or maybe I can dance for both of yall."

She headed over towards the bar when one of her regular customers pulled her down on his lap. She giggled, greeted him and took the ten out his hand, and then they walked to the private area together. The private area was for private dances and it was lined up with opened booths with couches. She sat her customer down and placed her booty in his direct view and started dancing.

When Chantel returned, Trey immediately turned his attention to her and didn't mention anything about Simone. He couldn't get the thought of a girl dancing for the both of them, or having a girl join them out his head; but he didn't know if Chantel would be down. He decided it was something he was going to have to ease her into and tonight they would just start with a private dance. He stood up as she returned.

"Before we leave, let's get a private dance together," he cheesed, hoping she would go for it.

"Whatever you want," she laughed. They stopped by the bar and got a drink first and spent about five minutes guzzling it down and flirting with each other.

The walked over to the private area and handed the bouncer a ten to get in. One of the girls grabbed his hand and pulled him through the booths towards an empty one. Chantel watched all the girls dancing in their booths as she passed each one. It was a lot of stuff going on back there and she couldn't help but be nosey. One particular girl caught her eye. She noticed she wasn't dancing, but her head was bopping up and down on the man's lap. She tapped Trey and pointed the girl out. He looked shocked. He immediately recognized who it was from her bikini colors. He let a slight laugh out and kept walking. The girl turned her face to see who was passing by and knew instantly she shouldn't have done so.

"Simone!" Chantel yelled at the girl.

She sat up quickly, wiped her mouth, nervously fixed her bikini top and pulled her hair back. "Oh hey Chantel! What are you doing here?" she asked.

She grabbed Simone by the arm and pulled her close to her. "You got to be crazy! I knew you were dancing but you in here doing tricks too?" she whispered in her ear.

Simone jerked her arm back and stepped back, "Look I gotta do what I gotta do. Everyone doesn't have a man to take care of them like you."

She sat back down next to her customer with an attitude and stared back at Chantel waiting for her to leave. She was embarrassed but wouldn't show it. Amazed at her attitude, Chantel threw up her hands and walked down to Trey and by this point was ready to go. She didn't want her dance anymore even though Trey was already getting started; she demanded they leave.

On the ride back to Trey's apartment he racked his brain trying to figure out why Simone would say that to him. Was she interested in him? In Chantel? Did she ever mention these desires to Chantel? What would happen if he bought it up? He decided to just let it go and take his mind off it. Chantel on the other hand was racking her brain trying to figure out why Simone would take that extra step and start doing tricks. She had to be making enough from just dancing; she didn't need to go the extra mile. I know Isis probably talked her into it, she thought. She also thought Simone was high but couldn't tell on what. She wasn't herself.

The next night Chantel decided to try to talk some sense into Simone. She opened the front door of her apartment and the smell of weed quickly traveled into her nostrils and settled in her lungs. She looked through the dim light of the slowly fading light bulb that sat without a shade in the lamp, and saw figures of four people. Once her eyes adjusted to the light she realized it was Simone, Isis and two men. What's new, she questioned sarcastically to herself.

"Come hit this," Isis said as she stretched her arm out to Chantel when she walked in.

She walked over and took what was left of the once long and thick blunt out of Isis hand. She pulled long and hard on it and let the smoke infect her lungs and handed it back. Isis handed it to the guy to her right who was sitting at the kitchen table with her. Chantel went in the bedroom and changed out of her clothes into a pair of sweat pants and a white T then returned to join them in the living room. She really just wanted everyone to leave so she could talk to Simone about what happened last night. It's been eating away at her since she saw it. It's not safe, it's unnecessary and she was getting worried about her. In a way she felt guilty because she started spending so much time with Trey, it left Simone to end up hanging with Isis.

The blunt got passed back around to everyone except Simone. Chantel looked closely over at her for the first time since getting home and realized she was high as a kite. She didn't need to go nowhere near the blunt. She laughed it off and hopped up to grab a bag of chips out the kitchen. She decided to just hang in her bedroom until all the company left, if they ever did.

"I'm gonna be in my room if yall need me," she said as she closed the door and plopped on her bed, flicking the TV on with the remote.

As soon as she got comfortable under her blanket, her cell phone lit up and buzzed. When she realized who it was, she rolled her eyes and hesitated on answering it. She just wasn't in the mood.

"Yes mother."

"Hey, you got a minute?"

"Yea, wassup." She reached over and turned her TV volume down with the remote.

"I'm back in Cali."

"I figured that's why you were calling, to tell me that," she sucked her teeth, "I don't see why you want to go back to that place with bad memories and the same old tired people doing the same old shit."

"Look, there was nothing out there for me in Jersey. You and your brother both left me there alone. I don't know anyone, and I don't really like anyone around there. So what was I supposed to do with myself? Just sit around and get old?"

"You could always try getting a job. Starting a new life. Doing something productive. You're going to run yourself in circles back there. Same shit again. And then expect someone to turn back and help you."

"I don't need your help! You forget that I'm the mother."

"Well you don't act like it with these dumb decisions you make."

"Damn Chantel! I get it. I was a screw up mom. I fucked up in every way possible. Do I need to hear it over and over? I fucked up. I did. I set you and your brother up for failure. He's in Jail and you're in NY doing God knows w—"

"Doing what? I'm doing perfectly fine. I'm good! I won't end up like you. I refuse to follow the same path you did, so don't put me up there with the list of failures," she cut her mom off.

"I'm just saying I know I screwed up. If you're going to throw it in my face every time we talk, then we are going to grow old and bitter with each other. It's time to let that shit go Chantel. How can I ever get right when you still talking to me like I'm some dope fein?"

"Because how do I know you're not?" she asked seriously.

"Fine Chantel. I can't prove nothing to you and I shouldn't have to. I'm your mother."

"Exactly! You ARE my mother. Don't act like I didn't spend my eighteen years of life around you. I know you. Don't forget that."

"Bye Chantel. I see I can't talk to you right now. You must be in a pissy mood." She hung up.

Partly frustrated with her daughters attitude but partly frustrated with the fact that she was right. She was a failure of a mother and she should expect this kind of reaction from her. Chantel had to raise herself and in the middle of doing that she had to raise her brother and take care of her mom. She was rightfully angry.

As soon as she started drifting off to sleep, her bedroom door opened. Chantel was a light sleeper and the slightest noise woke her up. That vice was a product of her upbringing. She was always prepared for the worse and always on guard. She saw it was just Simone and relaxed. Her red shot eyes caught her attention though. Damn she must be really high she thought.

"You good?" Chantel questioned her as she watched her look aimlessly around the room for something unknown.

"Yeah, I'm cool," she answered and walked over to Chantels bed. She placed one hand on her hips, "I'm just looking for my purse. You seen it?"

"Nah. Which one?" She eyed her suspiciously and began to think she was high on more than weed. Which that alone surprised her because she didn't even know when she even started smoking weed to begin with.

"The Louie bag. My favorite one," she said and leaned on her elbows on Chantel's bed, "I can't find it," she sighed.

"You high?" Chantel flatly asked.

"Naw. Just some drinks. Pulled on the blunt a little," she lied.

"I think you lying. I know someone high on some other shit. That's not just liquor and weed," she told her. "And you know I know."

"Come on, ain't no one doing anything. I'm just trying to find my purse," she defensively snapped back.

"It's not in here Simone. You need to check out there and see if that sneaky bitch got it."

"Dang why she gotta be all that?" Simone scrunched up her face and stepped back from the bed.

"Oh so we defending her now? I been calling her a sneaky bitch since day one. Now it's something new?"

"I'm just saying, you don't know she cool by now? You just need to hang out with us more, but you be too busy for ya girl now a days. You went and got boogie on us."

"Oh you definitely gotta be high because you talking outta pocket now." Chantel sat up in her bed.

"I'm not! Even if I was. Who the fuck cares," she said and turned to leave the room.

"You trippin." Chantel jumped out of bed and got in her path. "I don't know when you started talking reckless to me like I did something to hurt you but that shit needs to end right now. And you gonna sit here and defend that shiesty bitch Isis." Chantel reach over and closed the bedroom door so they wouldn't be in her business.

"Bitch please. You need to really get a hold on ya self. You think you better than us. Walk around like your shit don't stink. Isis is more a friend then you ever was," Simone spat back.

"Are you serious? You can't be. You can't even be serious right now." She stepped closer into Simone's face.

"I'm dead serious. I'm tired of you walking around here like your top bitch. Well look, I bank more money then you now, you can't boss me around no more." She started flinging her arms around and getting loud.

"Oh I see Isis got you brainwashed. When did I ever boss you around? I always looked out for you. I always made sure you were straight even when you ain't have shit of your own. You gonna calm this dumb shit down right now. You forget who I am?"

"I didn't forget. I know exactly who you are. A jealous hood 'friend' who think she better then everyone. Did you forget that your moms on drugs and your brothers in jail for killing her boyfriend....who rapped you?" She twisted her neck back and forth as she spewed fire at her.

Nothing else was to be said. Chantel started swinging landing each punch into Simone's face. Simone's reaction was to block the hits and she had no time to even retaliate any at Chantel. It was clear who was getting beat. Simone finally got a handful of her hair and pulled for dear life. It sent a pain through Chantel's head that caused her to slow the speed of her punches and try to get her hair free. She grabbed at the hand on her head and now threw kicks to Simone's gut. It forced Simone back and she tumbled against the dresser then to the floor bringing Chantel with her.

Isis overheard the noise as they banged into the dresser and then the floor and went to investigate the sounds.

"Are yall ok?" she asked as she tapped on the other side of the door.

No one answered it. She held her ear to the door and heard heavy thumps. She slowly opened the door and peeked in.

"Oh my God!" she screamed and ran up behind Chantel and tried to grab her arms, stopping her from hitting on Simone. "You guys are friend! Stop it! What the hell is going on?" she screamed and struggled to pull Chantel back. The two guys in the living room ran up to the door and watched as if it was their entertainment.

"Fuck her! I hate her," Simone screamed in tears as Isis finally was able to pull them apart. She pulled her shirt down to cover her exposed stomach.

"You a dumb bitch! Why you make me go there with you?" Chantel said as she pulled her hair back off her face.

"Yo! What happened?" Isis yelled, and looked back and forth between the two girls expecting an answer.

"You losing it. You really are," Chantel said as she bent down and picked up her sneakers. Breathing heavily in and out she struggled to catch her breath.

"Whatever. You're jealous."

"Jealous of what? You don't got shit! I'm the one with a good man! I'm the one who's going to college. I'm the one who got stacks! I put you on game a long time ago how to get money. You must have really lost your mind, thinking you have something I want. You're just a hoe who does tricks for dollars. Dirty bitch please!" Chantel yelled. She put her sneakers on and looked around for her cell phone and purse.

"Damn Chantel, ease up. What is wrong?" Isis questioned again.

"Ease up? Bit-" she stopped herself and took a deep breath. "You don't even know what's going on, so mind yours before I beat your ass like I beat hers."

"That's why I'm asking. I'm just trying to help," Isis replied, and rolled her eyes and turned away, "and ain't no one beating my ass."

"Don't try me," Chantel snapped and grabbed her purse and threw her cell phone in it. She went in her closet, pulled down her black Addidas bag and started going thru her closet and pulling out clothes.

"When you come off your high from whatever the fuck you was putting in your body, and you ready to apologize for this shit right here, then come holla at me. Until then I will be at Treys."

"Pshh. She said apology!" Simone said sarcastically to Isis and laughed.

"What really happened?" Isis asked for the third time, directly to Simone.

"She just dumb. She started by trying to say you stole my purse," Simone started to explain.

"What? What the fuck would I need to steal your purse for?" Isis got angry, "You said I stole her purse?" she asked Chantel.

Chantel sighed and shook her head as she turned around out the closet, "I said maybe the sneaky bitch got it."

"Sneaky bitch?" Isis repeated.

"Did I stutter?"

"Yo, really what is your problem? I didn't do nothing to you," Isis responded.

"Exactly she just a hater," Simone added.

"Well since we all in here talking real talk, then let me open my mind to yall real quick. Simone, you have lost it. You let this girl come up in your life and blind you with the material life she lives all in exchange for her damn soul. This girl got you dancing in the club where you turning tricks too! You doing drugs now, drunk every single night, don't got no man, ain't talk to your family in months, and you follow this whore around like she God," She spat and zippered her night bag up, "and Isis you have been sneaky since day one. Something about you ain't right and you don't have Simone best interest at heart. If you did, you wouldn't be bringing her down like this." She threw her bag over her shoulder and picked up her purse and keys. "You two nuts can have each other."

She stormed out the bedroom and out the apartment. The trunk of her car popped open, she tossed her bag inside and slammed it shut. Inside her car she sat silently evaluating what just happened. Her mind scrambled to put the pieces together. How did that just happen? Simone was her best friend! Her phone rang and it was the only person in the world she wanted to talk to.

"Baby, you won't even believe this shit I just found," Trey said immediately when she answered the phone.

"No you won't even believe what just happened to me!" she yelled back in the phone.

"I'm telling you, this is some wild shit. Your girl Simone is on some hoe shit," Trey responded.

"You ain't saying nothing new. You saw her at the club! I just got in a fight with the bitch! I had to beat her ass Trey."

"You beat her ass? Yall was scrapping? What happened, where you at?" he asked concerned.

"I'm sitting in my car about to come by your spot. We just got into it, and I told her about herself and Isis too. Bitches tried to gang up on me," she said and started her car.

"Damn ma, Hurry up and get here because I got something to show you."

She ran though the events in her head and couldn't believe how things happened. Her feelings were genuinely hurt. Simone had become like family to her and she never expected anything like this from her. The bond they developed all this time was suddenly broken. As she pulled up and parked on the street her throat tightened up. She reached up and wiped a falling tear before it hit her cheek. Ahhh, you buggin girl, crying over this, she said to herself.

The walk to Trey's apartment gave her a moment to calm herself down. She sniffled and rubbed at her nose one last time and knocked on his door. The overnight bag dangling on her shoulder got heavy and she switched arms. Trey opened the door with his laptop in hand. He wore black basketball shorts with a plain white t-shirt. Even though Chantel was an emotional wreck, she was temporarily sidetracked by the muscles that jumped out the sleeves of his t-shirt.

"Hey. Baby you ok?" he asked as he leaned in and kissed her.

"I just can't believe she came out her mouth at me. She was high! And I don't mean on just some weed, she was on some other shit." She plopped down on the black leather love couch in the living room.

"Alright before you tell me your story I gotta show you this. It's going to blow your mind." He sat down next to Chantel and placed the laptop in her lap.

Chantel immediately became alert as she looked at the screen and saw an escort site. She took a second and scanned over the page to figure out what he was trying to show her.

"Oh hell no!" Chantel looked more closely at the images. She rolled her finger over the mouse pad on the keyboard and clicked on the screen. "Trey, tell me my eyes are playing tricks on me. Tell me that is not Simone on this site."

"Yo, but the crazy part is that I don't even think she knows she is even on here. All these are like hidden camera videos on her profile. None of these girls are even aware and she looks drunk as hell," Trey said. He clicked on her video to show Chantel.

Simone was clearly high and or drunk; her body was flimsy and limp. Her limbs were not sturdy; she stumbled as she walked over to the bed. Isis walked over to Simone, who now sat on the edge of the bed and began to kiss her. She soon walked away, leaving her alone with a man. Isis never returned to the screen while Simone and the man began to get it in before it cut off short. It was only a two minute preview available.

"This is crazy! I knew Isis had her turned out!" Chantel said as she scrolled through to find any more videos but was unsuccessful. "I wonder if she knows! Look baby you gotta be a member/client to watch the full video. I bet Isis is caking off this site and Simone just got played into doing it. Not getting a damn dime." Chantel shook her head. "Look at this! She even got her 'modeling' pictures up here that she has been shooting with AJ. They been scheming on her all along."

"Isis is a beast," Trey said as he jumped up from the couch, "Oh so what happened back at your crib?"

"I don't even know. I just know that she was high babe! High as hell and she just started going off at me because I said Isis might have stolen her purse. She couldn't find it and I told her check Isis! She started defending her like she was her blood sister and what not. We just started going at it and she had the nerve to say some slick shit about my family and some stuff in my past that was just completely irrelevant. I had to dig in her ass. I just snapped and swung off on her. She probably still is picking her dippy ass off the floor," Chantel spazzed out, getting angrier as she told the story to Trey.

"Damn. I can't even believe that. Why would she flip on you for something so small?" Trey said as he closed the lap top and sat it on the round glass table that sat in front of the leather couch.

"I don't know. No idea."

"You gonna tell her about this site?"

"Hell no. Fuck her. She deserves this. She thinks Isis is her best friend, her homie, her sister. Let her keep playing her out, dragging her through the dirt and using her. I am not helping her anymore!" Chantel sucked her teeth.

"Nah. Don't do that. That's your girl. Yeah, yall fought but come on you can't let her go out like this. You seen that shit she into, she's on drugs. She needs your help. Talk to her tomorrow," Trey suggested.

"Nah, I pass," she said with an attitude.

"Well I can't make you, but I really think you should. Your just upset now, just sleep on it."

Chantel let the next five days pass without going back to her apartment or making any contact with Simone. It didn't seem to bother her on the outside but in the inside it was still hurting her that Simone would react that way over a simple comment about Isis. Isis was the devil in Chantel's eyes and she wished they would have never allowed her in their lives. She knew from the beginning she was trouble. Simone was just so naïve and let her get to close even after numerous warnings, Chantel thought disappointingly.

Trey decided to take matters into his own hands and try to talk to Simone. At least get her to open the doors of communication. He knew his girl wanted to make up and continue the friendship but that she was just too stubborn to step up first, especially when she wasn't the one who was wrong.

He walked hesitantly up to the apartment door and knocked. Isis opened the door but he expected Simone. "Hey, is Simone home?"

"Naw she went down the block to the store. She will be back in a few minutes though," she answered as she leaned on her right hip forcing her curves to be accentuated even more.

"Alright I will come back." Trey turned to leave.

"You can wait in here. She just went to pick something up. Should be back any second." She opened the door more to let him in.

"Nah I'm going to just come back." He turned to leave again.

"Alright well she gonna be right back. It's no use of you leaving," Isis replied. "Just wait here."

"I guess I can wait. She gonna be right back?"

"Yup."

He walked in and took a seat on the couch. There were music videos playing on the TV and Isis walked back over to the kitchen. The smell of fried chicken seeped out and made him hungry. His stomach started talking to him.

"You cooking chicken in there?" he yelled toward the kitchen.

"Yeah it's just about done. You can have some," she responded.

"That's what's good." He nodded his head in agreement.

She walked back and picked up her cell phone that sat on the table in front of Trey. He couldn't help but peer down her shirt when her cleavage was fully exposed as they spilled out the top of her tank top. She noticed his stare and smirked.

"So how is Chantel doing? After all that drama she hasn't been back home," Isis said and took a seat next to him.

He laughed in his head when she said home as if it was her home as well. "She's doing good. You know, just working on getting her classes in order for her first semester."

"Oh, she's taking classes?" Isis had no idea.

"Yeah she starts in a few weeks."

"You know what? I'm really upset with how things turned out. I never wanted Chantel and Simone to be mad at each other. I can't even believe it."

"I know. That's why I came by. I wanted to talk to Simone about it. See if I could get them talking again. It's been a week. That shit needs to be dropped."

"Yeah you right. But how you been though? I hardly see you around here anymore," Isis asked.

"I'm doing good. I just be busy. You know how it be. I stay working," he replied.

He checked his watch to see the time. He knew Chantel would be out of class soon and he wanted to meet her back at his spot with good news. He was hoping to catch her before she went back out.

"Yeah I know how that can be."

She rested her hand on his thigh and rubbed it. He looked over at her confused, and leaned over further away from her. He knew what she was trying to do as soon as she touched him.

"Relax. Ain't nothing," she said and slid between his legs on her knees.

"Isis you crazy. Get up. I didn't come here for this," he replied and sat straight up, ready to stand up and leave.

"No one has to know. It can be like old times." She stared up at him with her sassy eyes.

"Nah that's crazy Isis. You know I have a girl now. We said we would never speak about the past. So kill that shit."

"I do know, but I won't say anything to her, and you won't say anything to her. I haven't said anything yet." She rubbed her hand on his crotch and reached up and unbuttoned and zipped down his jeans.

He sat allowing her but was fighting it in his head. He knew Isis was a sex kitten and she oozed sexuality from every pore on her skin. He always lusted for her but he knew she was more like a forbidden fruit. He had it before and knew if he relapsed back to it he might get hooked again.

She began to reach in his pants and pull out his manhood when he came to his senses and stopped her.

"Isis I can't do this. I gotta go." He pushed her back, grabbed his pants up and headed towards the door. Just then Simone walked in and stopped in her tracks.

"Oh, hey Trey," she said unexpectedly. Her eyes went down to his unbuckled jeans, then over to Isis sitting on the floor. Her mind immediately went to assuming.

"Simone. I came by to talk to you. I gotta go now though, I don't have the time. I'll come by later," he said and made his way to the door. He left immediately.

"Um you need to tell me something Isis?" Simone questioned as she sat her keys and purse on the kitchen table.

Isis smiled her usual devious smile. "None of your business," she replied and returned to cater to her chicken.

11

~ Other People's Property ~

"Twenty, forty, sixty, eighty, one-hundred…twenty, forty, sixty, eighty, two-hundred," Isis counted to herself up to six-hundred. She folded the money and stuffed it back in her wallet, grabbed her keys and headed to the bank.

Money was coming in from all different avenues and she stashed and saved the majority of it. She loved looking at her accounts and seeing how much she has been able to accumulate over the last two years since meeting AJ. He was her right hand man, her ace boon coon, her lover and her business partner. They had a mutually agreeing relationship where they both knew money over anything. If it meant being with other men or women to get the cash, they allowed it. AJ played all his models in order to gain his trust, so he spent time with Simone. Isis not only knew all about it but she encouraged it.

Trust between them wasn't even an issue. It was like they were made for each other. They thought just alike and hustled in every situation they could. She knew that she could place her life in his hands and he would not only take care of it, but flip it and make a dollar out of it. The escort website was just one of their hustles. Constantly they were working, coming up with new ways to make any kind of money even if it was small money. Money is money and they aimed to get it by any means necessary.

As she returned from the bank, her phone got paged. She knew what that meant. Ricky, one of her suppliers of prescription drugs, had some pills to drop off to her. Good thing too because she had a few orders waiting to be filled, which meant money waiting for her. She hopped down the steps and out the front door. Anticipating him to text her with the location she began to stroll down the block towards her car. He hit her with the address and she jumped in her car to meet him.

"What's up lady?" Ricky said as he walked around the corner.

"Hey, hunny!" Isis responded. They embraced in a hug as she handed him a wad of cash.

They engaged in small talk as he handed over a small bag with her prescription meds. She headed off on her way to handle her daily business. The thought of poppin some of the pills herself crossed her mind but she fought off the strong urge with the even better thought of more money.

She wondered if Simone was home and decided make a surprise visit. Her car was out front so she didn't bother calling. There wasn't much to do today until evening hours when they both had to work at the club so they just hung around at the apartment. Isis had a craving for a harder drug then usual and decided it was the perfect time to put Simone on it as well.

When she arrived at Simone's apartment, she didn't bother asking; she pulled out a mirror and a razor blade. Simone just eyes her curiously even though she already knew what she was about to do.

"Whoa. Wait, what are you doing?" Simone stopped her.

"I'm about to pour this white on this mirror. Line it up. Roll this twenty up, and snort this substance up my nose," Isis replied truthfully.

"I mean damn. I didn't know you did that stuff."

"There is a lot you don't know. So now you do."

"What does it feel like?" Simone asked.

"It feels like drugs. What do you want me to say? Amazing? You won't know until you try it."

"Oh nah I am good. I just wanted to know."

"What you mean you good? I came over here to have company and company isn't fun unless their enjoying this pretty white stuff with me."

Simone turned her nose up. She couldn't imagine doing a drug this hard but her curiosity began to eat away at her. Not only did she want to find out what it felt like, she wanted to escape her reality as always. She felt like being as high as the clouds would help her get away from her feeling of being as low as dirt lately. She had a lot on her mind and decided to just go for it. Isis wouldn't let her say no anyway she thought to herself. Isis was satisfied with her decision.

"I got a problem," Simone softly said.

"A problem?" Isis gave her the most confused face ever.

"Yeah. A problem."

Isis eyed her new best friend oddly. No clue to what she could be talking about, she turned her body to face her fully. She prepared herself to hear something scary. Although she knew nothing was ever too big of a problem because she knew people everywhere and had connections all over. She hopped she was talking about the drugs she just took. Or else she would snap on her for being so damn paranoid.

"Ok, what's the problem?"

Simone hesitated, got up and headed into the kitchen. She returned with a bottle of vodka and a glass.

"I think I'm pregnant," she said as she poured herself some of the devils juice into the glass.

"Oh wow. Ok so first question is did you miss a period?" Isis responded looking confused.

"Yeah. Its two weeks late. On top of that I'm always nauseas in the morning," Simone said nonchalantly as she sipped the drink.

"Second question. Bitch why the hell are you drinking vodka then?" Isis snapped.

"I'm not keeping it," Simone said flatly.

"Dang girl. Are you sure about this?"

"Yea. I can't have a baby right now. To be honest I wouldn't even know whose it is."

"Damn, well if you want me to go with you to the doctor or if you need to talk, I'm here," she tried to comfort her.

Although Simone was very easy going about the situation, Isis knew she had to be somewhat upset. Being pregnant is not a simple thing to flag off the way Simone was doing and she hoped she really could handle it. Isis was as cold as ice but a situation like this made her sympathetic to a certain extent.

"Thanks. I will be fine." She grabbed her glass, headed into her bedroom and closed the door. Needing a moment of clarity and to be alone, she left Isis out in the living room.

When she returned out of her bedroom, Isis was gone and the apartment was silent. She wobbled over the couch and plopped down. She stared off to the blank white wall ahead of her beyond the TV. Her eyes focused on nothing. Her heart was empty. Her mind was blank. Her life was spiraling out of control and the main problem was that she didn't even realize it. Without any family or anyone to bring her back down to reality, her days were consumed with the paper chase and nothing else. Getting high was filling the void that she desperately needed. She hasn't spoke to her mother since the day she moved out and the lack of communication with Chantel slowly left her lonely and feeling empty.

She picked up her cell phone and made a call to a guy to bring her some weed. She needed to smoke a little before she headed to the club. He came right over and they rolled 2 blunts, smoked and she headed off to work. Being pregnant wasn't even a thought in her mind. She made herself believe it was nonexistent and planned to call a clinic first thing Monday morning to get it taken care of. At work she drank a few drinks and got lost in the music as she worked her way around the room collecting green bills.

At about 3am she finished up, collected her stuff and made her way to her car. She dug in her chocolate brown Louis Vutton bag and pulled out her cell phone. It blinked a blue light indicating messages; which were four missed calls. She stopped dead in her tracks when she saw the name under the missed call message. Mom. She racked her brain trying to figure out what possible reason her mom could have for calling. Since she left for NY they have not spoken and it wasn't by choice on Simone's end. She did attempt to reach out and call numerous times in the beginning but her mother just wasn't interested in talking to her. To see four missed calls from her mother at 3 m made her heart stop.

Slowly she picked her pace back up and walked to her car, got inside and sat staring at her phone. Not sure what to think. She hated her mother for never being there. She hated her for not showing any compassion. She hated her for the way she cut all communication. Even with all of those feelings she still was concerned. Deep down she wanted her mother.

Her mind was made up and she dialed her mother's number back. Her hand shook slightly as she pulled the phone up to her ear. The nerves were taking over her body, she wasn't sure what to expect.

"Hello?" Mrs. Hayes answered the phone.

"Mom, I got your missed calls," Simone spoke softly. She let go of the steering wheel after she realized her fingers where turning white from gripping so tight.

"Chantel called me and expressed she is concerned about you. I've spent the last four hours trying to figure out where I went wrong. I know I haven't always been there. I haven't always played a major role in your life, but I had my own issues that I let determine how I viewed you and our relationship. I regret it deeply. I love you Simone, you're my daughter. I hope you know that," Mrs. Hayes expressed all in one breath.

"Chantel called you?" Simone snapped, not expecting to hear that.

"Yes, she did. Is there something wrong? Are you ok out there, do you need help with anything?"

"No, I'm fine, what did she say?"

"She just said she's concerned with you, and that you are getting into stuff you shouldn't be involved with. She didn't give me details and I wouldn't expect her to. That is why I am calling you, to find out if there is anything I can do. I don't want you to be involved in the wrong things, you have other options, you do know that right?"

"I'm fine. I don't need anything. I don't know why you decide to care now. You never cared. Didn't you tell me never to come home?"

"Simone listen, I never really talked about this but I guess it's time for you to hear it." She paused. "When your father and I got married, I never wanted kids. I just never did. Your father so badly wanted a son. He pleaded with me to have a baby in hopes of having a little boy."

Simone rolled her eyes listening to her mother. She didn't like where the story was going. Knowing that she was unwanted wasn't going to make anything better she thought.

"I decided that if my husband wanted a baby I was obligated to bless him with one, even though I didn't want one. We got pregnant and found out it was a boy. During this time things couldn't have been better between us. My career was going well, your father was enjoying his teaching and we had a baby boy on the way," her mother continued.

"Wait, I have a brother?" Simone cut her mother off.

"No, you don't. I lost the baby with a miscarriage. It was devastating to us both but your father held a lot of resentment towards me for it."

"Why would he hold that against you? It's not your fault!" Simone snapped in confusion and anger.

"Back when I was just dating your father, I was also dating someone else. I contracted HPV from him and that affects your cervix and can cause cervical cancer. I had to have a surgery on my cervix where they slice out part of your cervix in order to avoid cancer.

Doing that also makes it difficult for you to carry a baby full term. That's why I miscarried."

Simone sat dumbfounded, she never had the slightest clue her parents went through this. Imagining the pain that they both had to experience in this situation hurt her heart. Then she thought about the baby in her stomach and squeezed her eyes closed. She fought the feeling of crying, she didn't want to be weak.

"After all of that we waited a few years and tried again. This time around we ended up with a girl. We were blessed to even have you but your father was still bothered that I couldn't give him a boy. My body couldn't handle trying again for a boy. He loved you so much, but he hated me for how things turned out. It kind of slowly tore us apart and the anger I had towards your father for blaming me, I took out on you. I have gone over and over this in my head; I even sought counseling at one point." She stopped talking. There was an awkward silence. Mrs. Hayes waited for her daughter to comment but Simone was speechless.

"In time I realized your father had to be cheating on me. Things were just different between us. I let it go on for a while, hoping things would get better. Hoping that he would realize it wasn't my fault and that I was still a damn good wife regardless of the situation. Things didn't get better though and I took that out on you as well. I felt like you were the reason my marriage was failing, when all along it was his fault for blaming me. He loved you regardless if you were a boy or girl but he took his disappointment out on me. My behavior was completely wrong of me. I was selfish and I know this now. I don't want to continue on the way we have been Simone."

She could hear her mother getting emotional through the sniffling. Still speechless for words, she shifted in her seat getting anxious to leave. She glanced at the time on her car dashboard and badly wanted to get home to her bed. She put the car in reverse and pulled out her parking spot.

"Are you going to say anything?" Mrs. Hayes asked.

"I don't know what to say. I really don't. I'm sorry you went through that but am I supposed to feel sorry that you treated me like crap?"

"No I don't want you to feel sorry for that at all. I am asking you for forgiveness. I want a new relationship with my daughter. Is that possible?"

Mrs. Hayes realized that she needed to help her daughter because she was obviously going through something. The only way to help her was to build a relationship with her and she desperately wanted to. She was more than shocked when Chantel contacted her; she never expected that.

"Of course." Simone said. Although she didn't really want much of a relationship with her mother at this point, she also wasn't going to fight it.

"Ok, I'm going to hold you to that. Get some rest. I love you and will talk with you soon," her mother said and it almost sounded real.

Simone has never heard her mother speak like this and it actually made her uncomfortable to hear mother express so much emotion. "I love you too," she replied.

It made her feel even more uncomfortable express it herself. She wondered what Chantel said to her mother to make her react so drastically. First thing in the morning she had a trip to make to Trey's apartment to see Chantel. This had gone on too long and she was ready to sit down and talk with her.

In the morning, Simone rolled over and opened her eyes. She squeezed them tightly as a pain took over her head and pounded nonstop.

"Ahh, my head," she moaned and sat up on her bed. The liquor she drank the night before dehydrated her brain leaving her hungover. "Shit," she spat.

As soon as she stood, there was a knock at the door. She slid on her flip flops, walked past the mirror and glanced at her appearance. Her black mascara was smeared under her eyes, gold shimmer shadow sparkled over her face, and her hair was a tangled mess. She ran her hands through it to tame it but it didn't help much. She walked over to the door and pulled it open. The instant she did she regretted doing so.

"Rent is past due. I need the money now," Mr. Hattie said sternly.

He stood with his hands on his hips. The summer heat created little trickles of sweat on the deep dark skin of his nose. The v neck white t-shirt clung to his solid brown body and exposed the top of a tattoo that spread across his chest. Simone thought it was sexy as she eyed it. She let her eyes roam down to his blue jeans that fit just right. Mr. Hattie was an older man but he still held onto his smooth youthful sexiness. Simone imagined him in his younger days to be such a ladies' man.

"I thought it was paid. Chantel told me she paid Mrs. Hattie two days ago," She lied as she leaned on one leg poking her hip out. Her right butt cheek slid out from under her light blue cotton boy shorts. From the angle she stood she made sure it was visible to him. Simone knew the power of her body.

"I don't believe she did. I checked before I came by here. It's not paid," he answered. His eye strayed from her eyes to her erect nipples that poked through her wife beater. He couldn't help but look and it was almost impossible to ignore them.

"That's what she told me. Is there any way I can check with her and check my bank account and get back to you?" she asked with a slight pout.

"I really need the money Simone. It's already late and this isn't the first time." He felt bad to have to be so stern about it to such a beautiful girl but it was late constantly.

"Ok well come in for a second. I'm going to call Chantel because I know I was told it was given to your wife. You can come right in for a second." She stepped back and allowed him to enter.

Hesitantly he walked in and took a seat on the couch. She turned and walked over to the kitchen table to get her cell phone. A slight grin formed across her face because she knew he was staring at her ass cheeks as they bounced around when she walked. She turned around to face him and caught his glace. He quickly raised his eyes to hers and shifted in seat, knowing he was caught looking.

"Excuse me while I call her."

Simone opened her phone and pretended to call Chantel. She held the phone to her ear and waited then pretended to hang it up. "No answer." She slid the phone back on the table. She took a seat next to him and he immediately stood up and faced her.

"Look, the rent isn't paid. I'm going to need the money by the end of the day, or tomorrow morning I'm going to have to serve a formal eviction," he said as he looked down at her.

The crazy thing was, that she had the money to pay the rent but to let the money go on something like rent was a waste in her opinion. She would much rather use it towards a new Gucci purse or something to further intoxicate her mind. Her priorities were so backwards that it was normal to her at that point.

"Look, is there anything else I can do? Any other way I can pay you for now? For the month?"

She reached out and slid her hand slowly in between his legs up his inner thigh. He jumped a little at her first touch but allowed her hand to travel up to his package. He closed his eyes and imagined how much he would enjoy screwing her.   She didn't react immediately because she wasn't sure how he was going to react. She wanted to be sure that he was down with it before she pushed it on him.

"There are other things besides money," she said peering up at him from the couch.

He stood silently still. His muscles in every part of his body were tense. As much as he wanted Simone, he knew he shouldn't. He was having an angel and devil on the shoulders moment. Simone didn't mind one bit sleeping with him because he was a smooth older man. He wasn't ugly and she has dealt with far worse on some late nights at the strip club. She knew that this would be the only way to make him forget about the rent for the month at least. She used her sexuality to her advantage whenever possible. She even hopped she put it on him so good she never had to pay rent again. She knew her capabilities and what she could do with the power of the pussy.

"Uh. No Simone I don't think that's a good idea. You know I'm married," he said and stepped back from her reach, "I just need the money."

She rose to her feet and walked so close to him her breast pressed against his chest. He allowed it, even though he wanted to step away he didn't.

"Just let me make you feel better. You will forget all about the money," she insisted.

She grabbed his hand, moved her shorts to the side, and pulled it between her legs. Took his finger and slide it through her lips and inside her. Her moist muscles gripped his finger and she leaned her head back and let a soft moan out. He couldn't resist anymore. He slid his tongue up and down her neck and in a circular motion. She didn't want him to really get to kissing her and such. She just wanted to make him bust a nut so she could send him on his way.

She dropped down to the floor and began to unbuckle his jeans. He ran his hands through her hair and grabbed a handful. With his now exposed penis he guided himself into her mouth. She slurped slowly making sure to wet the whole shaft. Taking full advantage of the situation he roughly pumped in and out causing her to gag a few times before she could continue. He enjoyed taking control and held firmly on to her head as he thrust in as deep as he could.

Unexpectedly the halfway opened front door was pushed all the way open. Chantel stopped in her tracks and stared. "Um you could at least do that in your room," she said in disgust and rolled her eyes. She looked closer and realized it was her landlord.

"Oh Mr. Hattie?" she questioned.

"Uh, hey Chantel. I was just…I was just leaving," he stuttered out and began to bend down to reach for his pants.

"Charles! What the fuck is going on?" Came an angry woman's voice as Mrs. Hattie bust through the apartment doorway. "I come down to collect rent and you got your pants down to your ankles!" she screamed.

By this time both Chantel and Simone are backing up away from the surreal event about to unfold. Simone wiped her mouth and smirked a little at the thought of him getting caught. That's what he gets, the trifling dirt bag she thought to herself.

Mrs. Hattie walked right up to him and started swinging, landing a few solid blows to his face until he could grab her arms and control them. The anger she felt for the situation came out both verbally and physically. The screams and commotion caused a neighboring tenant to exit her apartment and find out what was going on. She peeked in from across the hall and saw Mr. Hattie holding his wife with his pants down. Her face scrunched up in confusion at the scene and her eyes then wandered to the far left of the apartment. Spotting Chantel and Simone standing there watching the episode intrigued her even more. The girl had no problem being nosey; it looked like such an interesting conflict.

"I can't believe you!" Mrs. Hattie screamed as she tried to free herself from his grip. "You know what, let me go. Let me go. I'm fine. Let me go." She settled down and breathed deeply.

He slowly loosened his grip from her. Not sure if that was a good idea he stepped back. "Baby, would you just calm down for a second, please," he pleaded.

Mrs. Hattie ignored him and turned to the two girls. If looks could kill, they both would be six feet under and on the way to their maker. It was almost like steam was shooting out her ears and fire was breathing from her mouth. Mad or angry were not the words to even explain her demeanor. Simone rolled her eyes at the thought of a confrontation with this older woman. It was not worth it to fight over a man she didn't want. She just didn't want to pay rent.

"You young girls have no respect. Disgusting. Just disgusting. I want you to think about what you've done. Seriously think about it. This is my husband your down here trying to sleep with. You got thirty days to get the fuck out of here. Expect a formal eviction letter in the morning." She took a glimpse at her husband who was buckling his pants finally and stormed out the apartment.

"What the fuck you looking at," she spat at the woman hanging out her apartment door watching the drama as she stomped off to towards the elevator. Mr. Hattie hurried out after her; the nosey woman returned to her apartment and shut the door.

Chantel strolled pass Simone with her nose in the air. She didn't expect Simone to get this low but then again she did. All she could think about was how simple and innocent Simone used to be. Sometimes she thought it was her fault for bringing Simone into the world of greed. Money was all Chantel thought about at one point but once she had enough and lost the things that meant the most to her, it meant absolutely nothing to her anymore. Once she found true love and a man that cared for her and would never deceive her, the money was secondary. At least she thought so, because he had money and she had stashed away money. Simone on the other hand had no real stash. She saved a little here and there but majority of her money was spent on clothes, name brand purses and shoes.

Simone didn't know what to even say to Chantel. This was the first time she has seen her since their fight. She watched as Chantel took a seat on the couch and just stared at her. It seemed like neither one of them knew what to say. Simone walked over and sat on the couch also.

"So you fucking landlords now?" Chantel said with a blank face.

Simone wasn't expecting that. She thought they would talk about their friendship, apologize and try to mend things. Her guard went right back up and she sucked her teeth.

"I wasn't fucking him," Simone responded.

"Sucking his dick, giving head, fellatio… It's all the same," Chantel said.

"What is the problem? I haven't seen you in weeks so why come over here just to talk shit."

"I actually came to talk to you about some things, and to squash this beef because you need some help. I walk in and see you sucking off the landlord. Come on Simone you just letting yaself go, and for what?" Chantel got animated in her speech, using her hands to express her disgust in the situation.

"Don't worry about what I do. What does it matter to you whose dick I'm sucking?"

"It just got US evicted," she yelled back at Simone, emphasizing on us.

Simone sat silent. Unable to come up with anything to say she stared down at the floor. Her eyes wandered to her toes and she admired her fresh French pedicure she got yesterday.

"You're whoring ya self out. Period. Just straight getting out of hand," Chantel warned.

"Listen I don't need you telling me I'm a whore. Save that."

"No. Someone needs to tell you. You need to hear it. You're whoring yourself out," she repeated, "Get your life together, seriously. It's not a good look what you're doing. And that bitch Isis, does not have your best interest at hand. Watch her, she's sneaky as hell and you have no idea what she's capable of."

The rage was building up in Simone. In the past she always let Chantel talk to her anyway she wanted to. She looked up to Chantel so she always wanted to please her. Things were different now. Growing up and having to handle things without Chantel around forced her to build a small amount of courage. Although, most of that new found courage was backed by Isis usually.

"You act like your shit don't stink!" Simone yelled, "You were the one who put me onto using my body to get what I want. You were the one who fucked them dudes in your hood to get everything you ever had up until Trey came along and saved your ass." She rolled her eyes at Chantel. "You swear you got everything going on so perfect now cause you got a man. You can't even keep ya man from straying," Simone blurted out.

"What the fuck does that mean?" Chantel jumped up and leaned in Simone's face. "What you mean? I got a damn good man!"

"All I'm saying is you're not perfect. You don't got it all together as you would like to think," Simone said viciously and smirked.

"If you got something to say, then just say it. Stop this beating around the bush. We ain't children."

"Trey ain't a good man. He likes to get his dick sucked just as much as Mr. Hattie." Simone was now enjoying pushing Chantel's buttons.

The second the sentence left Simone's mouth, she regretted it. A swift jab to the jaw almost sent her to a black hole. She flew back against the back of the couch and grabbed her face. Chantel didn't continue to hit her like she wanted to do, but she backed up and stared at her. The same look Mrs. Hattie had just a few minutes earlier now took over Chantel's face.

"You fucked with Trey?" Chantel demanded a straight answer.

As much as Simone wanted to keep playing with Chantel's emotions, the pain from the hit was pulsating through her head and she could hardly find the words to speak.

"No I didn't fuck him. I never said I fucked him damn!" Simone whined.

"Then what are you saying. I'm not playing. What do you mean by he's not a good man and it's not perfect?" Chantel stood there breathing heavily like a bull. Ready to tear Simone up at the slightest comment that made her believe she had slept with her man.

"I'm Just saying that you come off to me like your life is perfect and it isn't. Your man is not perfect, you are not perfect. So don't judge me or look down at me."

"So now you want to switch up your story. Just a minute ago you were saying he likes to get his dick sucked just like Mr. Hattie. Simone tell me the fucking truth." Chantel was about to lash out on Simone. Her emotions were taking over. She knew exactly what she meant by the comment but she couldn't get Simone to confirm it.

"It has nothing to do with me," Simone said as she sat up on the couch.

She opened and closed her jaw trying to ease the pain from the punch Chantel just served her. Chantel got real close to Simone, so close they could smell each other's breath. She had a menacing look in her eyes; a look that would make anyone want to tell the truth, get out her way, and get on her good side. Simone decided to do just that. She knew what Chantel was capable of. She has seen Chantel whoop a bitch ass on many occasions and she did not want to be on the receiving end of that yet again. She knew she was on the losing end of this. Without Isis to back her up she really couldn't stand up to Chantel. At first she thought she could but it was just a false sense of courage because in reality she knew there was no way.

"Tell me what you meant by it," Chantel said calmly to Simone. She grilled her with her eyes. Looking for the slightest reason to jab her again and this time keep going.

"Look, I don't know anything but I did walk into the apartment and Trey was here with Isis," Simone gave in and revealed.

She knew Isis was going to hate her for running her mouth but she felt like her back was up against the wall since she let the original comment slip to begin with. Chantel wanted to beat the living shit out of Simone but she knew it would be pointless. She felt disrespected and betrayed by not only Isis but by Simone for not telling her this information immediately. Regardless of the little beef they had, she still considered Simone a friend and would expect her to tell her something like that without having to threaten or beat it out of her.

She stepped back away from Simone, giving her personal space back. She went to her bedroom and sat down on her bed that she didn't see in so long. Her emotions were a big wreck right now. She didn't know what step to take next. Leave Trey? What would her life be without him? Beat Isis ass? That was already on the list of things to do. Find somewhere new to live? She dreaded that and knew she would have to have a better income other then with relying on Trey. Her life just seemed to fall apart in that very moment of realization that she had nothing. That easily her happiness was taken away. She cursed herself for allowing a man to define her. She knew better that this.

She sat silently trying to come up with a plan and begin executing it. The feeling of helplessness was one that Chantel could not stand to endure for long. She experienced it sporadically at times in her life but never let it overcome her and she wasn't about to start now. She hated Trey that fast. That quick she wanted him to die for what he did. She didn't even know the details of what happened between him and Isis but anything involving that whore was a negative in her opinion. She decided to call him. Pulling out her phone and dialing her number became increasingly difficult with every second that passed.

"Hey babe," he said as he answered the phone.

"Trey, I'm going to ask you this once and I want to know the truth. Don't you lie to me."

"What's wrong?" Trey asked confused. His heart jumped because he had a feeling he knew what it was. Simone walking into what looked like a cheating situation was the worst thing that could happen to him.

"Did you fuck around with Isis?"

"Aw man, are you serious right now? Are you really asking me that? I don't want no parts of that hoe. I would not do that," Trey responded

"So why do I hear something went down with yall?"

"Where did you get that from?" he asked already knowing the answer. He didn't know if he should reveal that she came on to him and that he denied it. Or should he reveal their secret past together, that they used to fuck before he met Chantel. He didn't know how much she knew and wanted to keep her in the dark about as much as he could.

"That doesn't matter. If I find out you fucked with this bitch, it is over. Don't let me find out." She ended the call and sat there in anger.

He called right back repeatedly but she ignored the calls. Her emotions need a break and talking to him wouldn't help. Her next move was to figure out how to get herself more income and her own apartment. She knew she wasn't ready to let go of Trey but this was the first sign of betrayal and she was going to be prepared if any other skeletons came out.

If she knew anything about life, it was that you can only depend on yourself. Fuck friends and fuck boyfriends. She grabbed her bag and headed out for apartment hunting. She wanted something small and simple. She knew she couldn't afford anything lavish right now but planned to build herself up. There wasn't anything she couldn't do if she put her mind to it and she knew this. With the power of her beauty, the strength of her mind, and the influence of her personality she always set her goals high.

By the end of the day she ended up with a small one bedroom apartment. It wasn't anything fancy by far and she was saddened that she had to downscale her lifestyle but she knew it was what she needed to do at the moment. No way would she continue to depend on Trey because she didn't trust him anymore. She wasn't prepared to fully let go, but she now had her guard up. Her first move was to start packing. As she started to get her things together she did a lot of thinking. Her mind was racing trying to figure out what her plan of action was going to be. Where her money was going to come from was her number one thought. The idea of having to grind again for money made her miserable.

Her conclusion was that men where her only option until she could figure something else out. She just wouldn't let it take over her life as it had done back in Cali and she damn sure wouldn't let it consume her like it did to Simone. She was stronger than that.

It would be a bit more difficult because Trey was in her life now but what other choice was left. Getting a regular job was just not going to be enough to support her. Working part-time for 8 dollars an hour was just not even an option. No way would it be enough to pay her bills and survive. Rent and school were her biggest bills and they were mandatory.

As she packed, she noticed Simone sitting on the couch, just texting on her phone. She wondered where she planned on going. Mrs. Hattie said she would have a formal eviction notice in the morning, which would give them thirty days to move out. Chantel didn't even want to wait that long. She refused to be around Simone, Trey or even see Isis. She knew it would only be more drama if she took her time with leaving.

"So what are you going to do?" Chantel finally broke the silence between them.

"I'm not sure yet." Simone looked up from her phone.

"Well you got thirty days, but I'm out in the morning."

"You staying with Trey?"

"Nah. I got my own spot."

"Oh really?" Simone asked, secretly jealous. How did she get it together that fast she thought? She always envied her go getter attitude. She saw it in Isis and she saw it in Chantel but it just wasn't in her.

"Yea," Chantel responded proud of being able to handle her own when needed.

The awkward silence returned between the two. Neither one attempted to talk anymore. Chantel did what she had to do and that was to leave Simone hanging. It was time for Simone to be her own person without her. She was disgusted at the person Simone had become and had already said her peace at trying to help her. I'm not her damn mother, she mused to herself. Even knowing that Isis was the master manipulator, Chantel still couldn't let her pride down enough to really extend a helping hand. It hurt her so much when Simone took Isis side over hers.

The next morning Chantel decided to pay Trey a visit before going to her new apartment. Not only did she need to talk to him she needed to gather her belongs that acquired over time at his spot. He has been calling her phone all day and night trying to reach her but she ignored every single call. As soon as she arrived and knocked, the door swung open.

"Where the fuck you been at?" Trey stood there with an attitude and waited for an explanation.

"Just like a man to turn the tables on the woman. What are you mad about?" She asked as she walked in. The skin between his eyebrows was wrinkled and his lips poked out causing him to look like the grince who stole Christmas.

"I been calling you all yesterday and you just now showing your face around here." He followed her into the bedroom. She never stopped to face him and talk, she continued the task at hand; gather her stuff.

"Look. I'm not feeling this shit I been hearing about you and Isis. So I'm gonna go clear my head and find out the muthafuckin truth. Then maybe we can have a discussion about where I been," she snapped back. She reached in the closet and pulled out hangers of clothes and threw them on the bed. She reached back in the closet for more.

"What the fuck are you doing?" Trey grabbed the clothes out her hands and tossed them back in the closet, "I already told you the truth. I don't want that girl! Fuck her."

He stood in her way of the closet, not allowing her to retrieve anymore clothes.

"I don't want to argue, so stop yelling at me. I'm going somewhere else until I feel that I know what is going on. Right now all I hear is words coming out your mouth. It doesn't mean it's real," Chantel calmly said.

She moved away from him and gathered her makeup, put in her makeup bag and zipped it shut. Trey stood watching helplessly as he watched his girlfriend pack her things and collect them on the bed.

"Baby why would you believe someone else over me? Who else in this world got your back more than me that would make you believe them?" he solemnly said.

She froze. That last comment stung her heart because it was sadly the truth. Chantel had no trust for anyone at this point. The one person she thought would hold her down and that she could trust is the main one she was questioning. It blew her mind how life seemed to always blow her in the wrong direction and there was nothing she could do about it. No ones left she thought. No one. She was about to burn the last bridge she had left with anyone. The sadness turned in to anger. Good riddance she mused as she angrily grabbed her bags, walked them over to the door and threw them down.

"Yo I'm not letting you leave like this," Trey said and grabbed her by the shoulders on her second trip to the door. She dropped her bags and screamed.

"Get your hands off of me!" Tears rushed down her face and she instantly broke down. She attempted to wiggle free of his grip but she went nowhere. He pulled her in close to his chest.

"You're not leaving me," he repeated over and over as he held her.

He knew she didn't want to go. Chantel let all her bottled up emotions about her mom, Simone, Trey and Isis out. They stood in completely silence accept for the sniffles and the heavy breathing of Chantel for close to five minutes. He knew she was overwhelmed with things and that's the only reason she let someone get in her head about Isis. Still unsure of how much information she actually knew, how much was true or how much was false, he didn't bother to ask. He would of course just deny, deny, deny.

Trey really loved her; he eventually wanted to marry her. It was just a matter of being ready. He wanted to be out of the drug game for good and still able to support for her and a future family. His savings were enough to take care of them for a long time but he knew he still needed to have more money coming in if he stopped. His mind started working that very second on a plan. He knew he wanted to marry her and make sure she could never think about just getting up and leaving again. He wasn't having it.

12

~ By Any Means Necessary ~

"Hurry up and take the shot, we are late!" Isis yelled down the hallway to the kitchen.

Simone emerged from the bedroom, in a pair or sweats, a wife beater, and black and white Jordans. "I took it! Stop rushing me."

The two of them headed out together on another night of paper chasing. They jumped in Isis' car and sped off to make up for lost time. It was a miracle they didn't get pulled over on the highway because Isis was speeding and swerving in and out of lanes like she was in a race. Cutting cars off and tailgating was the only way she thought she could make up for lost time and could get to the private party in time.

Once they arrived, Isis quickly made her way to the front door of the house while Simone took her time behind her. She already had three shots and smoked a blunt before they departed so she was feeling good and relaxed. In about an hour she was going to want to pop some pills to mellow herself out even more. Her routine was becoming worse and worse going from just liquor to including all types of drugs. Cocaine had also become a drug of choice for Simone.

Inside the front door was an immediate change of atmosphere. The relaxed, calm and laid back Isis had to instantly turn on to head bitch in charge. The men were all sitting around, lounging drinking beers, eating chicken wings, playing video games and listening to the stereo blast Young Jeezy. All eyes were on them, as they headed to a back bedroom to change. Isis could just see the dollar signs that seemed to be dancing in each man's eyeballs; "cha ching" she thought. She could hear the excitement from the men as they slapped hands and talked about how fat the girl's asses were as they walked by.

Around the room each man got prepared for what was to come. They made sure their money was right before arriving because they were told tipping was necessary for attendance. This wasn't a bachelor party or anything like that; just a few buddies decided to throw something together just for pure fun. Eric the owner of the house was a basketball player overseas and was just returned home from a six month season. His friends decided that this would be a great way to welcome him back to the states. Eric stood a tall six-four with a lean yet muscular build. You could tell he was an athlete by his physique but not to mention the ice that draped around his neck. His brown skin complexion was acne free and smooth. When he smiled, his pearly white veneer teeth capture your attention.

"What's taking them so long? I'm ready to smack some asses," Eric said anxiously. He gulped down the rest of his beer and threw the bottle in the recycling trash can in the kitchen.

"Forreal. I'm 'bout to check on them hoes," his long time childhood friend Roscoe said.

Roscoe was the total opposite of Eric. He was short, stocky and nowhere as fresh as his friend. He developed a husky build after serving eight years in prison over armed robbery charges. The attractive young man he should have been was taken away through his hard life. He grew up in the hood where you were either a drug dealer or a ball player. His height only left him with one option or else he would be playing alongside Eric on the court. Through it all they still remained good friends.

The lines in his face told a story of hardship and the scar hidden beneath his chin was a reminder of his life almost being taken away from him. While in prison he was attacked and almost had his neck sliced wide open in a struggle. Luckily for him the makeshift knife missed the crucial part of his neck and just sliced right under the chin. He was grateful for his life but wasn't scared to lose it. The way he saw it was that everyone was going to go at some point so there was no point fearing the inevitable. He felt like he was living a hell on earth anyway.

Roscoe walked over to the back bedroom door to check on the ladies. He didn't bother knocking on the door and poked his head right in. Simone was lying on the bed and was in a two piece black bikini with a pair of black stilettos on. Isis was in a hot pink two piece bikini, sitting on the edge of the bed and was talking on her cell phone.

"Yall ready?" He asked.

"Give me a second, I'm on the phone," Isis answered.

"Naw, we don't got all night," Roscoe shot back in hiss usually ignorant tone, not liking the fact that Isis didn't jump when he expected her to jump. He was a man used to getting his way.

"Well I have to finish this phone conversation. So either you're going to wait or we can leave," Isis responded with an attitude, making sure he knew she wasn't a back down type of girl.

"Who the fuck do you think you talking to, bitch. Yall not going nowhere until you hoes dance," he stepped inside the bedroom.

This was one of the few parties they attended without AJ as their "bodyguard." Unfortunately he had an important shoot to do and couldn't go with them. They thought they would have it under control. With the raised voices and foul language, Simone rolled over and sat up. She was zoned out from the drugs and liquor but took notice to the tense nature of the conversation.

"Look. I ain't about these games. I'm almost done. Either you give me a second or we can leave now and call you some other girls from the club to come dance for yall."

Isis was frustrated but knew she didn't want to push this man's buttons to hard. Plus she knew pissing him off was only going to hurt her pockets in the end. He walked over to Isis, grabbed her arm and looked her dead in her eyes. Isis didn't know what this man was capable of but didn't let her fear show either. Simone got up out of bed realizing this was about to be an ugly situation. She eyed Roscoe cautiously trying to figure out his next move. She admired the muscles jumping out his bicep as he held onto Isis. It was almost like she couldn't help but notice and appreciate them. There was a big tattoo that read "Live to Die," and right under in smaller print said "I'm ready." Right below it in even smaller print it read "Take me now." It made her wonder what type of life he lived to want to glorify dying.

"Let go of my arm," Isis said calmly, keeping her composure.

He realized his temper was getting the best of him and shoved Isis back lightly and let go. Isis walked over and immediately grabbed her jeans and began to pull them on.

"Get ya shit. We outta this bitch," Isis snapped as she pulled on her shirt and slide on her flip flops. Simone quickly followed suit.

Roscoe already made his way back to the living room by now. As the girls walked out the bedroom fully clothed the men instantly sensed there was a problem.

"Yo, why yall dressed? Where yall going?" one of the men shouted over the music as he stood up.

"We out. Some of ya friends don't know how to act," Isis responded and continued to the front door.

"Naw, didn't we pay these bitches already, Eric?" Roscoe jumped in.

"No you did not pay us yet. Fuck you," Isis snapped back

They left the men standing there dumbfounded and exited out the front door. All of them were familiar with Roscoe's temper and knew he had to have said something to offend them when he was checking on them in the back room.

"Can you believe that shit?" Isis asked as they made their way to her car.

"Yeah, he was out of line. Real Talk," Simone responded.

"You're not gonna be grabbing me the fuck up like that. Not this bitch."

They headed back to the car. Isis was thinking about how they could make up for a nights loss of money. She couldn't bear to just go home and sit there and not be productive. Either make money or meet men with money. They decided to head to the club, but first stop back at Isis house to change clothes. As they pulled up to Isis home, Simone stared intensely at the exterior of it. This was the first time Isis bought Simone to her place. She lived right outside of the city in northern New Jersey and never spoke about her spot.

"I usually don't do this. I like to keep my place of living to myself, but you cool. I trust you," Isis said and turned the engine off.

Once they entered, the front entrance was lit up by a beautiful chandelier. Inside the color theme was red, black and white. Everything matched from the carpets, furniture, curtains, and table settings. There was a big painting and white sculpture design in the entrance hallway. Against the back wall in the family room was a set of three black leather couches forming a curve around the room. A glass coffee table sat in the middle and in front was the flat screen TV.

Simone took a seat on one of the couches and continued to admire the quality of her house. Everything was top notch. Nothing in her home looked cheap or as if she bargained shopped for it. The house was damn near a mansion in an uppity neighborhood. She had no idea she was making money like this. Simone wondered how stripping was affording all of this. They made good money but this was just too lavish. Isis went back to the bedroom and emerged with a new outfit on. She handed Simone something to put on as well.

"Here. Put this on. The bedroom or bathroom is back to the right." She motioned over to Simone to go change in the back.

"Thanks." She headed back to the bedroom.

"Yo, your house is beautiful," Simone gushed as she returned.

"Thanks. Business is good. What did I tell you? Scared money don't make money and hunny I ain't never scared," Isis joked.

"This house is just crazy. Let me use the bathroom before we go." Simone ran back to the back.

Isis sat and waited when he phone began to ring. She quickly searched through her purse to locate it and caught it just before they hung up.

"Wassup?" Isis spoke into the phone.

"Got bad news. Some detectives came by here today. They were asking questions about our site and the dating service. Doesn't look good at all," AJ replied.

"Are you fuckin serious? What did they say?" Isis mood suddenly changed.

"They just asked a lot of questions. Seems like their investigating it along with other things. They wanted to know who where the people in the videos, did we have consent forms, what where their ages, where they paid, and asked did our girls have sex on the dates. Stuff like that. I made sure that we looked like a real dating business as much as possible but I don't know how to hang on to these lies. We have to prepare ourselves."

"Shit! I got Simone over here now; I'll call you back later tonight to talk about it."

Isis closed her phone and all kinds of thoughts ran through her mind. Their website was illegal as hell. Most of the girls on the videos didn't even know they were on video. There was always a hidden camera or they were to drunk or high to realize it was there. Some of the girls saw the camera but just didn't care. They had no idea it would be put on a membership website or else they would be asking for their cut. Some of the girls who were down with the escort service were ok with having sex for money but were unaware of the website and the profiles with videos.

After the thought of possibly going to jail ran through her head, the thoughts of how much income she would lose without the site up now took over her mind. Perverts were paying twenty-nine ninety-nine for the first two months and nineteen ninety-nine for every month after. These men loved amateur or homemade porn. Majority of her money was from this site. The members had the opportunity to book dates with whatever girl they wanted on the site, as long as they could convince the girls to go. Dancing was doing her good, private parties were also good, and pushing prescriptions pills was great, but the site was constant money coming in with little to no work. AJ and she were filming at just about every private party she danced at and that she bought her girls to. She was even featured on the site herself a few times. Whenever work was slow and she didn't have any video updates, she would feature some of herself at the parties. Isis had no shame in her game. As long as she was able to afford any and everything she wanted, she didn't care.

Simone came out, dressed and ready and Isis tried to get her mind focused on just having a good time. She was instantly stressed with that phone call. Either way she looked at it, she needed to make a huge come up on money. Whether it was simply to support her lifestyle or to afford a damn good lawyer, money was now on her mind times ten.

Isis decided the best place to spot money makers was a high elite type of club. She made sure to pick a spot that she knew there would be men with money in attendance. They drove up to the Pink Elephant and pulled into the valet parking. One of Isis regular customers at the strip club was a bouncer of the club so they were able to avoid the long line of wanna be in girls waiting to get picked to be let in.

Once inside Simone headed straight for the bar, and Isis followed with her radar on full effect. She knew that none of the men around the bar really had the big money. All of the big spenders were in VIP buying bottles not drinks. She scanned the area until she saw where the VIP sections were. After both purchasing a Long Island, they made their way to the dance floor. Simone was sipping and two stepping to the beat, feeling the music. Isis finally relaxed and just let her guard down; she wanted to enjoy herself for once instead of worrying about money. Her mind was a constant stream of cash, it was just her nature.

Isis drank her drink unusually fast. She needed the relief. Simone's drink was still teetering at the top of her glass and she sipped it constantly trying to bring it lower. Just then someone bumped into her back forcing her to drop the glass on the floor. Luckily the glass didn't break but her liquor was wasted all on the floor and dripped down her leg.

"Damn, excuse you," Simone yelled as she turned around and saw a huge six-five, two-hundred and twenty pound big black man. He was huge.

"Damn lil'mama. My bad. I didn't mean to bump you," he said, holding up his hands as if to say it was an accident.

He instantly noticed her beauty and her sexy figure. He used this situation to get to talk to her. "Did it spill on you?" he asked and grabbed her hand, pulling her to the bar. She shook her head yes with an attitude. He grabbed a few napkins and ran them down her legs, trying to wipe off the spilled drink.

"Thanks," she said annoyed.

It was like all that Isis or Chantel had ever taught Simone about men had gone out the door. All Simone was worried about was wasted liquor and how it delayed her getting drunk by even just a few slight moments. Her addiction to the drink had become so bad she didn't even realize it. It blinded her sense of money. She looked at this man and just saw an asshole who spilled a drink on her instead of someone with a lot of money. Her money radar must have been broke.

"What you drinking on? I'll get you another one," he offered.

She scrunched her face up thinking about what drink she wanted. Something strong she thought. Another long island was the best bet to get her feeling the buzz she so desperately wanted.

"Matter fact, I have bottle over in VIP, I was just on my way to the bathroom. If you want you can just go over there and tell them that Kenny said yall good. I'll be over in a few.

Her face lit up and she finally got a better look at him. She admired his smile; his teeth were pearly white. Her eyes were suddenly drawn to his yellow diamonds necklace that draped around his neck. How did she miss that to begin with, she wondered to herself. Dollar signs went off in her head as she took a full look at his physique, style and jewelry. She knew he was a football player from that alone. She took a quick mental note of his name and flashed him a smirk.

"Alright, I'll be waiting for you." She walked off back to Isis who was dancing in front of a guy. Simone grabbed her arm and pulled her away from the stranger and headed to VIP.

"What happened, where is your drink?" Isis questioned.

"In VIP," Simone replied with a smile.

Proud that this time it was her doing that got them behind the red ropes. It was almost like a competition between them. Who could get the men with money first was always the happy one at the end of the night. Simone was sure excited about her opportunity. On top of all of that, she enjoyed his physical appearance; he was fine. He was big and stocky, very athletically built. His dark complexion was smooth as a baby's bottom and his smile was perfect.

By the end of the night the two new love birds were saucy and couldn't keep their hands off each other. It was clear they both wanted to go leave the club and handle business but Isis advised against it. She knew that he could be a good pay off along the way if she strung him well enough. Don't give it to him too fast and play your cards right she advised.

"Nah hold out. Not the first night. You gotta keep him around for a while. Get paid every week like it's your job," Isis whispered in her ear.

"I hear you," Simone slurred back and waved her off.

She was in her own world and didn't want to hear anything. Although she knew Isis was right, her judgment was fully impaired. She was on a mission and that was to satisfy her appetite. The thought of riding his assumed big chocolate penis and holding on to his masculine biceps had her wet like the Nile River. Every possible position ran through her head as she sipped her drink and danced in front of Kenny. He sat back in the plush couch and watched her move. He admired every inch of her body and couldn't wait to slide in her.

He reached out and grabbed Simone; she landed on his lap. She giggled and leaned in to hear what he was about to say to her. Being careful not to spill her drink she held it out in front of her. Isis watched them in a jealous yet silent rage. Although she was happy that one of them had met someone, she was infuriated that it was Simone who snagged him first. His friends didn't seem to be on the same level as him. They looked like maybe cousins or friends from before the football days. None of them dressed as well, had any ice on or had the athletic build of a NFL player. She was bored with them immediately.

Once 3:30am rolled around, Isis was tired of playing third wheel and was ready to go. She leaned over to drunken Simone and yelled in her ear that it was time to leave. Simone told her new beau she was ready to bounce and the three of them got up. Kenny went to each of his three friends, slapped hands and said his goodnights. On the way out the club, Simone dug in her purse for her valet ticket.

"I can't find the ticket," Simone whined.

"I have it," Isis said annoyed.

Kenny could sense the tension in the air with Isis and knew she was ready to go. A hater, he named her in his head. He figured he would get together with Simone when she wasn't with her bitter jealous friend.

"Cockblocker," he said under his breath.

Isis went in her bag, pulled out the ticket and walked it over to the valet man. She stood over by the curb waiting for her car to be pulled up, while Simone and Kenny hugged and said their goodbyes. Simone stumbled her way over when the car was in sight.

"I'm so drunk!" Simone said as she plopped down in the passenger seat and closed the door.

"I can tell," Isis still had an attitude.

She usually isn't the jealous type but she was pissed that she got no man tonight and Simone did. Her ability to pull men was never an issue and she didn't want to think that Simone could ever be her competition. She knew she looked better than her and had more game then Parker Brothers. The attitude wouldn't go away though, even after trying to push the whole night out her head.

Dropping Simone off was a relief to the end of her night. She sped off and headed home to her bed with an attitude. Simone wobbled up to her door and dropped her keys at least three times before she could get them in and unlock it. Once inside she flung her heels off and fell into bed. She didn't bother taking her dress off or wrapping her hair up. Her mind wandered off to the thought of the football player she met. She wanted him.

Her body was feinin' for him and there was a party down below in her panties just at the thought of him inside her. Her purse was still in her hand so she emptied it on her bed in an attempt to find her cell phone. She called Kenny. No answer.

The tingle down below intensified as she rubbed two fingers between her lips slowly. Moist and warm she slid them deep inside. It sent a chill up her spine and she let out a low moan. She knew she had to have someone else to come satisfy her urge. The next number she called belonged to AJ.

"Hey. What you doing?" she replied as soon as he answered.

"Just got in bed; was at the club. What's up?" He asked.

"Can you come over?" she asked.

"You do know it's after 3am?" he laughed.

"Yeah but that don't matter. Come over. I want to see you."

He agreed and was on his way in no time. Simone somehow got herself together enough to take a quick shower, throw on some grey sweat pants and a light blue tank top before he arrived. The second he walked in her apartment she was all over him. Her hands were everywhere on his body and tongue was soon to follow. He wasn't even able to shut the door before she almost had his pants off. Of course he didn't question or stop it.

They stumbled into the couch as she pulled off her sweat pants. They both were naked from the bottom down. She straddled him, licked her fingers and rubbed it in between her legs. Then grabbed his penis and guided it inside as she hungrily rode him. As soon as she got a good rhythm going she locked up grinded deeply into him. Orgasm after orgasm came and she slowed her ride down. He lifted her up, got behind her and bent her over. Entering from the back was his favorite position. He grabbed her hips and pounded deeper and deeper with each thrust in.

Her appetite was fully satisfied and she waited for him to finish. She lifted her head and turned to the right to see Isis standing in the doorway. Damn caught again on the same couch, she thought to herself.

"Isis?" She stood up and pushed AJ back off her.

"Yeah I see yall. Been standing her for a while watching," Isis said calmly.

AJ stood speechless in a state of confusion. He couldn't tell if she was mad or wanted to join. The original plan was to win Simone over in the first place, in order to get her on board with going on the escort dates. But Isis stood there watching so calmly with no reaction, not like any other girl would have. He didn't know how to read the situation but pervert brain was hoping that she just wanted to join.

"I ain't even mad. I expected something like this to happen. My fault for letting you think it was cool to smash her in the first place. Where are the cameras AJ? I thought we agreed only for work," Isis said and turned and walked towards the elevator.

She wasn't even going to argue, get mad, or start any drama. She knew she really had no place. They weren't a couple, or in a relationship, and she talked to other men often. But they had an agreement and a mutual understanding that if there was to be any fucking for pleasure it was with each other. All else was work purposes and he always knew when it went down. AJ even had access to her money so he knew when she was working or not.

"Cameras?" Simone questioned AJ.

AJ ignored her and grabbed his pants. As he put them on Simone walked to the door and looked out. Isis was gone that quick.

"That was weird," Simone said as she shut the door, "What is she talking about?"

"Nothing. I don't know what she talking about." He grabbed his keys off the table and headed to the door. "I'm about to get out of here. I'll get at you later."

"Oh. Ok." Simone was hurt. She didn't know what Isis was talking about and why AJ had to rush out. She wondered what kind of relationship there was between Isis and AJ. She thought they were always just friends but it seemed like more.

Simone shrugged it off and got into bed. She quickly dozed off into a deep sleep and woke late in the afternoon to a phone call from Kenny. A smile crossed her face as she pulled the phone up to her face. His deep husky southern voice made her excited.

"Hey lil mama," he said as she answered. "Did I wake you?"

"Yeah, it's ok though. What's going on?"

"Just wanted to see if you wanted to grab something to eat later tonight?"

"Sure, what time?"

"I get out of practice at five. So is six good?"

"Yeah I can do that."

"Ok cool, I'll hit you later then."

The rest of the afternoon she spent trying to figure out what to say to Isis. She wanted to call her but was nervous to hear her reaction. Confused and afraid she finally decided to just send her a text. Hoping that she could avoid conflict at all cost, she simply just sent a message that said 'Hey girl…what's going on?'

About fifteen minutes later she finally got a response that said 'just chillin.' It didn't really let her know if she was mad or not, but the shortness of the message made her think she was mad. After sitting there staring at her phone for five more minutes, she picked it up and just called her.

"Hey. I just wanted to see if everything was ok. What was up with last night?" Simone asked.

"Oh nah I'm good. I actually just came by to check on you. Make sure you didn't slide out with that football player. But obviously I saw you were busy."

"Oh. So what was that camera and agreement stuff yall was talking about?" Simone just had to know.

"Nothing girl. It wasn't nothing." Isis played it off. She didn't feel like explaining anything to her and wasn't in the mood to make up lies.

Simone accepted the answer because she really didn't have a choice. She smelled a big bucket of bullshit but decided to ignore it. Her guard was now up against Isis when it never was before. In the end Simone knew that Isis was her girl so she tried not to think anything of it. She just knew she wouldn't do anything to hurt her.

Later that night, Simone went out with Kenny. They immediately hit it off and the vibe between them was instant. After dinner they sat for an hour and a half and had drinks and talked. She had to call it an early night unfortunately because she had to work at the club tonight. On her way to work she popped a few pills and drank a few shots. Getting loose before work was a mandatory thing at this point. With everything going on in her world, her escape was simply get high. 'Fuck it' she mused to herself as she hopped out her car and made her way through the back parking lot to the side door of the club.

"Hey. Hey," a loud voice called as a shadow jumped out a parked car in the lot. Simone turned in reaction to the voice. She strained her eyes but couldn't make out the figure. She hugged her bag close to her body and kept walking.

"I said hey! Hold up for a second." He sped his walk up towards her and she sped her walk up away from him. Once she got to the door of the club she turned around to look again. He still was following her. 'Who is that?' she thought to herself.

"I just wanted to meet you. Damn you gonna run away from me? I'll just holla at you inside then," he said with an attitude.

He got close enough for her to make out his face. It looked familiar but she couldn't place it. Was it one of her regulars at the club? Just someone she's seen on the street? One of Isis friends? She racked her brain trying to figure out why she thought she knew him. As he got closer she stepped in between the door frame and just barely stuck her head out, in preparation to dip in the club quickly. She still wasn't sure who this man was or what he wanted.

"I ain't going to hurt you. Relax. I was about to go in the club and I saw you. I just wanted to come check you right quick," he said as he approached her at the side door.

"I'm saying. Its dark out and it's an empty parking lot. I gotta be careful," she replied and leaned on the door frame

As he approached she finally realized where she knew his face from and her mood turned sour. Ready to slam the door shut in his face she hesitated when she realized she would have to see him inside the club as well. Remembering his feisty attitude, she reached her hand in her purse and grabbed her key chain. Her mace gripped tightly in her hand she stood by the door and waited for him to get close.

"I don't want no problems. Just your number. You fly that's all." He stood admiring her cute face.

"I don't think I should. You don't remember me?" Simone questioned.

He squinted his eyes as if that would help him remember. He couldn't figure it out and gave up.

"Nah. I don't know ma." He shook his head.

"You was coming at my homegirl. We were supposed to dance at your boy's party the other night." She prepared herself for a negative reaction.

He scrunched his face up as he flashed back to the half naked girls in the bedroom that he was ready to bash their faces in.

"Oh yeah I remember now." He sucked his teeth.

"So what now you don't want my number?" she said with an attitude. She really didn't want to give it to him anyway but she found it funny that he switched his mood up on her.

"I still want your number…but you now owe me a dance," he joked.

She smiled for the first time. "Oh really? I owe you a dance?"

"Yeah you do. A lap dance. Oh yeah and with that same little bikini you had on when I met you." He shook his head up and down picturing her in the bikini. "Come on. You need a man like me around in your life anyway. Then you wouldn't be dancing up in this club. You would only be giving me dances at the crib."

She giggled, let the mace and keychain fall back into the bottom of her purse. His aggressive charm was rubbing off on her and she was ready to give him her number. He pulled out his Iphone and unlocked it.

"So whats up. Let me get that number. Get you out this dusty ass club."

"Here." She reached out and grabbed his phone. After she put her name and number in she hit save and handed it back. "Well, I gotta get inside."

"Ok ma. I will see you in there. You know I was serious about my dance?" he said with a smirk.

She laughed and closed the door. Actually, she was happy to have run into him again. Even with him being such an asshole to Isis at the party, she was drawn to his confidence and aggressive demeanor. He seemed to demand whatever he wanted and it turned her on. All night she avoided him in the club because she actually was nervous around him. She had an instant crush and didn't have one of them in a long time. Her nerves were getting the best of her, so she masked them with liquor. Shot after shot went down between dances. By 3am she was way too drunk to even work her last hour on shift.

"Simone. Your drunk, get yourself home. Get in a cab," Daddy said as he stepped outside his office. Simone walked past and stopped.

"I'm ok. I can stay," she slurred out. She tried to focus her vision on her boss.

"No you're drunk. I can't have you stumbling around my club. You're an easy target. Get yourself a cab home," he demanded.

She rolled her eyes and sucked her teeth. She knew she was drunk but thought she could handle one more hour. After changing her clothes she headed out front to hail a cab. She definitely couldn't even attempt to drive. As she was waving down a cab, Roscoe left the club. He immediately noticed her and went over to offer her a ride to her apartment. He made sure she got home safe and tried his best to respect her. He really wanted to see her again.

Isis wasn't working that night but she stopped by the club to collect some money from one of the other dancers who owed her. On her way out she was stopped right in her tracks.

"We need to talk," Nadine said to Isis as she approached her.

"What's up girl? Everything ok?" she questioned.

"Nah It ain't at all. I been hearing that when I work these jobs on these dates that you taking a lot off the top without telling us." Nadine stepped closer into Isis personal space.

"What? Where you hear that shit from? You know I take my ten percent and give yall the rest," Isis lied.

"Look I know you bullshitting me. I been talking to my clients about my fees and they been paying way more than I'm getting minus the ten." Nadine started to get aggravated.

"I don't know what you're talking about," Isis replied with an attitude.

In that exact moment, Nadine wasted no more time talking. She jabbed Isis right in the lip and the two girls started going at it in the middle of the parking lot. Two big bodyguards from the club ran out and tore the two women apart but not without a struggle and handfuls of hair being grabbed.

"Isis I want my fucking money! Every last dime! Get my shit to me! This ain't over, I promise you," Nadine yelled as she struggled to get out the hands of the body guard. "Let go of me!"

"Fuck you, Nadine! I was helping you out! You needed my work to put food on your table for your daughter! Fuck you!"

"Don't bring my daughter up. Just have my money or I'm going to have to take it from you. I'm going to see you again either way," Nadine spat and walked away fixing her shirt and hair. She hopped in her car and peeled off, leaving Isis standing there with all eyes on her.

"Fuck yall looking at!" she shouted and walked to her car embarrassed.

13

~ Roscoe's Rage ~

"Baby." Roscoe rolled over and kissed Simone on the neck, waking her out her sleep. She moaned.

He pulled her up against his body, and ran his hands up her thighs and rested them on her hips. She squirmed at his touch and could feel his manhood growing hard, poking her in the butt. She knew what he wanted. The two of them had been going at it like newlyweds since they met just two weeks ago. It seemed to be perfect for Simone. She met a guy she liked, and needed at the same time.

With all the drama going on between her and Chantel and their landlord, Simone needed a place to stay ASAP. Roscoe had no problem offering his space for her to crash in until she got her plan finalized. Within the blink of an eye, she had packed and moved her stuff into his apartment. Sprung after two weeks she was falling quickly. They spent every day together since they met and their friendship was tight.

The one thing she made sure of was that Isis didn't find out who she was seeing. The way he disrespected her at that private party, Simone knew that Isis wouldn't approve of Roscoe. And her approval meant a lot to Simone. She was still under her wing in a sense and wasn't emotionally stable enough to stand on her own two feet. It was clear that Simone was a follower and as long as that person was willing to lead her, she would be willing to follow.

After mind blowing morning sex, the two of them got dressed and went to a diner to get breakfast. He told her that the rest of the day he had to work so he wouldn't see her until tonight. He gave her his key to his apartment and mandated that she make a copy and be home when he gets home tonight so he can get in. She had no problem following his directions and was happy to have her copy of the key finally.

As they were leaving her phone vibrated, displaying the name Kenny. She knew it would be a bad idea to answer in front of Roscoe so she canceled the call and sent it to voicemail. He noticed her actions but didn't say anything. He let it go this time but knew if he suspected her dealings with other men he would speak up and claim his property. He already marked his territory.

Once she got back to Roscoe's apartment, she had absolutely nothing to do. Her relationship with Isis had been weird ever since the AJ incident. Isis hasn't said anything negative and said that everything is ok but her actions show it differently. She hasn't heard from her in a few days which was odd. She hasn't heard from AJ either but that's not that farfetched. She only heard from AJ every few weeks anyway. Her relationship with Chantel was completely broken. They haven't spoken in a few weeks and she was curious how she was doing. She wanted to bury the hatchet and try to at least be cool again. The tension between them was slight because they both had their hands full with their own issues and problems. But in a finally sober mind, before she drank anything or popped any drugs, Simone decided she wanted to reach out to her. It took her a good twenty minutes before she picked up her phone and called her.

They decided to meet up and have lunch. Chantel arrived first and waited patiently as she nibbled on bread and butter. She ate two pieces before Simone got there and took a seat across from her. Their first exchange was dull and timid on both ends. They both didn't know how to react to each other or what to even say. A simple hey was all that left their mouths. Simone picked up the menu, scanning over to find her selection. Chantel reached down and pulled up her lap top and powered it on. Simone watched her in confusion.

"I just want to say I'm sorry. I never meant for our friendship to go south this way. I hope that we can forget the past and maintain being cool," Simone blurted out, getting uncomfortable with the awkward silence.

Chantel stopped and looked up. A little shocked by what she said but relieved that she finally got the guts to apologize. Much appreciation was given in her head and she instantly accepted. Letting her guard down she spilled her feelings too. She let her know how she felt about her, Isis and every detail about why she didn't like

Isis. When she got to the part of the website, Simone didn't want to believe it.

"How would she have video of me and I didn't know about it. I would have seen a camera," Simone argued.

"Obviously you didn't. You were probably too high or drunk. I'm telling you that I saw it. I even showed Trey. Did she ever try to get you to go on random dates with guys?" Chantel said and at that very moment her laptop finished loading. She went into her favorites and clicked on the website. All she got was an error message.

"She must have taken it down," Chantel said as she tried to refresh the page. Still no luck.

"I don't want to say you're a liar, but there is no site and she never tried to get me on dates. Wait once she told me she had this old guy I should go on a date with but that was right before me and her kinda had an issue so I haven't spoke to her about it again," Simone said.

"See! There is a site. I wouldn't make this up. You know that's not even my style. At least I hope you know. It was up; it must be down right now. She has an escort service! I'm telling you," Chantel tried to convince her. "They even had your modeling pictures on there. They are playing you! Straight using you."

Simone sat in silence trying to comprehend everything Chantel was saying but it still wasn't sitting right with her. She knew that Isis was a little controlling but never expected her to be using her in this manner. She couldn't believe it and she wouldn't believe it. Chantel closed her laptop after another three unsuccessful tries to load the website. In the back of her mind Simone knew that Chantel was right, especially after hearing AJ and Isis talking about agreement and some secret shit the other day when she caught them fucking. Simone was just in denial.

"I'm just telling you what it is. You don't have to believe me. You can keep hanging with that bitch all you want. At this point, it's not my life and I warned you. Do as you please," Chantel said getting frustrated at Simone's naïve state of mind.

"I mean I hear you. I really do, but I just don't see it the way you do. She has done nothing but help me. If it wasn't for her I would have no money. I'm living cause of her."

"Are you kidding me? Living because of her? She got you shaking your ass and passing tricks for dollars. You not living. You are sinning!"

"Oh now I'm a sinner? So you went and found God now. Holier than thou Chantel. Please save that bullshit," Simone sucked her teeth.
"I didn't mean it like that. I'm not perfect. Not at all, but I do know that this bitch got you acting all out of character. I've been trying to look out for you but you just don't want to hear it."
"You're exactly right! I don't want to hear it. I don't see it the same way as you. End of story. Get off it. Why can't you and I remain cool and still disagree on Isis? What should it even concern you?"
"Fine. Fuck it. I won't say anything else about the hoe." Chantel gave up. "So on to something else. How's the love life been?" she smirked.
Simone immediately blushed, "Well, I'm talking to two guys. I like them both a lot!"
"Ok playa playa!" Chantel joked.
"Well you know how I do," Simone laughed. "One is Roscoe. He just cool as hell, he has this crazy swag to him. He just sexy to me and he really digs me. The other guy is a football player. I can't take him serious cause I know how they do. They have women all over and I know I'm just in line with a number. But we do have a good time together and I haven't been with a man with money like this ever! He just spends and spends, like its infinite."
"You got you a baller! If you don't feel it's serious then, I hate to say it but he probably using you so why not use him! I mean if he paid like that, there shouldn't be no problem with him throwing you some money here and there. Get in where you fit in," Chantel suggested.
Chantel knew what she would do with the situation and that was take full advantage of it. She knew Simone just didn't know what to do with such an opportunity. All she could think about is the shopping sprees she would be going on and the cash he would be handing over to her. She put herself in Simone's shoes for just a second. Enjoyed the daydream but was snapped back to reality when Simone asked how was Trey.
"Oh he is good. Actually he is doing really well. He is starting to get into this music scene heavy. He just opened his own studio and is working on his producing. He also got this rapper he is managing and it looks like he's going to get him signed to Def Jam. He's been back and forth to their offices, having meetings about the contract. So

hopefully that will work out for him, that way he can stop selling these drugs and shit. It's time to get out of that game. It's good but it's too good. It's bound to come back and hit him in the ass any second," Chantel explained.

"Yeah I know what you mean but damn that's hot. Def Jam is a good look. So what has been going on with you besides that?" Simone asked.

"Not much really. I am taking college courses now. I'm trying to eventually get my Bachelors' in Public Relations. Trey is going to start his own label and hopefully I will be able to assist in that with what I learn. We are trying to really pull this off, its grind time baby. Bonnie and Clyde style," Chantel boasted.

By the end of lunch they were laughing and catching up like old times. It seemed as if they both let go of hard feelings and just enjoyed each other's company. The only disagreement was about Isis and they agreed to disagree and to leave in alone. Finally things seemed back on track with the two. They went their separate ways and promised to hang together again soon. Simone decided to not say anything to Isis about the website or anything until she could see it for herself. She didn't want to start any friction between them and accuse her of something that doesn't even exist.

First thing she did when she got back to Roscoe's apartment was fall into the bed. She rolled over and relaxed, exhaling deeply. For some reason she was exhausted and the bed felt so good to her. She pulled her purse up and dug in, pulling out a small pouch. Inside were her pills and she needed one badly. The feeling it would bring her would put her comfortably in a nice state of relaxation. She grabbed a half empty water bottle and swallowed one, washing it down with water.

Her mind ran wild with the conversation at lunch today. She tried not to upset herself with thoughts of Isis being shady and using her. Her thoughts actually stayed on Chantel. She felt herself getting sort of jealous. Envious of how much she and Trey were accomplishing and their togetherness. This feeling wasn't new to Simone; she always held a small amount of jealousy towards her friend. She sort of looked up to her.

Her phone rang. She looked at the number but didn't recognize it and hesitated to answer it. Once she decided to answer it she regretted it almost immediately. It was a bill collector, for her MasterCard that was three months past due. She rolled her eyes at the thought of paying them money. She hung up on the customer service agent and put her phone on silent. She didn't want to be bothered by them for the rest of the day. They called often and she needed a break.

She hopped out of bed and grabbed the vodka bottle. She poured a shot and took it with ease. Her body was used to drinking liquor straight so it took no hesitation anymore. She wanted to forget about MasterCard and letting her mind relax was the way to do it. Or so she thought. She saw her phone lighting up out the side of her eye and she knew it was them calling back. She walked over and glanced at it. Yup same number, so she cancelled the call. She just didn't have the money to be giving to them at the moment. Even though she made good money dancing, sometimes it just wasn't enough for her lifestyle. She was at a point where some nights she would have good money and others nights, not so much. Her spending habits were out of control and a grasp on reality and responsibility did not exist to her.

Roscoe walked in unexpectedly and caught Simone off guard. She jumped up from the couch and headed towards the front door to see who walked in. Her face showed her confusion as he approached. He leaned in and kissed her on the cheek and went straight to the bedroom.

"Baby, I thought you were coming home tonight. Everything ok?"

"Yeah, I just had to get something I forgot," he replied. There were little wet spots on the shoulders of his jacket, so Simone assumed it was raining outside.

He grabbed something out his top dresser drawer but she couldn't see what it was. She walked over to be nosey and he sensed it. He quickly turned to face her; he didn't like anyone on his case being nosey. In his mind, that was her stepping out of line.

"What you forget?" she casually asked and leaned on the bed. She admired his physique from his shoulders on down. Her excitement about him still hasn't faded. She was infatuated with everything about him. She smiled to herself but that didn't last long as she was immediately taken by surprise by his blunt response.

"Da fuck? Is you my momma?" he snapped at her as he turned to face her.

She straightened up and twisted her face in confusion, "Babe I was just asking."

She rolled her eyes and started to walk out the bedroom. Clearly he was in a bad mood and she didn't want any parts of it.

"You walking away from me?" he questioned.

"What's your problem? Why are you snapping at me? I didn't do anything to you."

"Now you're talking back. You gotta learn this early and you're going to learn this now. Don't question me and don't talk back to me," he said as he walked up to her.

He got close to her face and grabbed her by the neck, throwing her up against the door. Her eyes bulged out her socket in fear, she gasp for air and tried to pull his hands away. "You got that?" he asked with an angry sneer.

She tried to answer but with his hands around her neck she couldn't get it out. Shaking her head up and down was useless as well because she couldn't move it. Still, he anticipated an actual answer and held on longer. She stared into his eyes; blood shot red and wondered what caused him to flip. Once he realized she wasn't able to reply, he loosened his grip, and pushed her up against door, letting go. She fought for breath and inhaled and exhaled deeply.

He walked off out the front door and slammed it. Simone slide down the door to the floor, holding her neck, trying to catch her breath. Tears streamed down her face as she sat in a state of confusion and sadness. She wondered what she did to cause him to get so angry but couldn't figure it out. After five minutes on the floor, she gathered herself and stood up. Still sniffing and wiping tears from her cheeks, she walked back over to the vodka bottle. It wasn't even 6pm and she was already taking shots and popping her pills.

After two more shots she laid out on her bed and cried. She didn't know what to do with herself other than just cry. She let it all out. She cried for every night she danced on a pole. She cried for everyday she didn't speak to her mother. She cried for the broken relationship she and Chantel had developed. She cried for the lack of stability she had in her life and how quickly her money went. She cried for the man she thought was going to be a part of her life but just ruined it.

Soon she forced herself to stop and grabbed her cell. She scrolled through it until she came across Kenny's phone number. She needed to get her mind off of everything and the only person who held no baggage with her was Kenny. They made plans to do dinner and a movie so she spent the rest of the day shopping for something to wear. Her wardrobe in her closet was enough but she wanted something new. She knew Kenny was used to having beautiful women around him all the time and she wanted to make sure she ranked at the top of the list.

She strolled through the mall, going in and out of stores. She wanted something casual but sexy, and not over the top. Her decision came down to a nice pair of jeans, pumps, and a cute top that showed just enough cleavage. Her mind wandered back to her closet to what purse she would carry and she decided on her newest Gucci bag. Shoes were not an issue because she already owned a few different style black pumps. So jeans and a top were on her agenda and maybe some jewelry.

Finally she found a pair of BEBE jeans that fit her curves perfectly. They were a light denim and slightly worn for one-hundred and fifty-eight. She found a gray and black shirt that she loved in the same store for thirty-eight dollars. After she bought the two pieces she decided to stick to some jewelry she already had at home. The prices of the jeans and top were out of her budget but she had no buyers' remorse. Looking good was a number one priority to her and she would do it by any means necessary.

On her way out the mall she stopped in one last store to check their earrings. Even though she knew she didn't need to spend more money, she couldn't help herself. She spotted a pair of earrings and a chain she liked and decided to take advantage of her five finger discount like the good old days with Chantel. She successfully removed them from their barcodes and backing and slid them into her purse. Unnoticed, she maneuvered her way out the store and made her way back home. By that time her high was wearing down low and she decided to wait until after she got showered and dressed before she took anything else.

She pulled up to the valet at the restaurant and ran to the door under her umbrella. The rain picked up and was now pouring. They had dinner at a nice Italian spot, since pasta was her favorite. The movie was next, but he suggested going back to his house and watching a DVD instead of going to a theater. She obliged and off they went. When they pulled up she was immediately amazed. The driveway alone was a long twirling drive up to a huge house that looked like something you only saw in movies. There were five small steps that led up to the huge front doors.

Once inside she was in awe of the beautiful design of the house and furniture. It was breathtaking and never in her wildest dreams did she ever imagine to be in a mansion of this caliber. Her mind ran wild of fantasies of one day living here. Sitting around all day playing housewife, cooking and cleaning while Kenny was at practice, ran through her imagination. Lounging around in satin PJ's, lying on the suede tan couch watching the movie projector screen as a TV, with no cares or worries except when the new line of Gucci hang bags was being released.

They headed downstairs where there were huge fish tanks built into the wall when you first entered. It was filled with small colorful fish and a neon light filling the tank from the back, making their colors stand out even more. Pretty she thought. As they turned the corner there was an unconventional all white pool table, with balls scattered across the table. On the other side, were some couches and a love seat, the sat in front of the flat screen. Kenny plopped down on the couch and turned on the TV, and Simone sat next to him. He knew she had to be impressed with his house and was very proud of his possessions and accomplishments. His confidence was on ten and knew he was setting the standard.

After the picked a movie, they snuggled in each other's arms and enjoyed the comedy they selected. Unfortunately every couple minutes his phone went off, whether it was a text or a phone call he was picking his phone up. Simone was dealing with the same problem as well. Roscoe was blowing her phone up but she ignored it each time. She wasn't sure if she should ever answer again after what he did. In the back of her mind she knew she would forgive him, because he was all she had. Right now she wanted to play the tough girl role and ignore him. Even though she had strong urges to answer she didn't all night.

By the end of the movie, they both downed three glasses of wine. He poured the last of it into her cup and stared at her with a smile.

She smirked back, "So you're trying to get me drunk?" she laughed and shifted in her spot on the couch.

"Naw, never that," he smiled, "Unless you want too."

They were interrupted by her phone lighting up wildly on the coffee table in front of them. They both looked at it and back at each other.

"You can answer it. I saw it lighting up all night. It's cool," he assured her.

"Ok. Excuse me." She picked her phone up and walked over to the bathroom and secluded herself for some privacy.

"Hello?" she asked.

"Where the fuck you at?" Roscoe yelled into the phone.

"I'm out. Why you worried about it. I don't fuck with you right now," she spat back into the phone, being careful not to be too loud. She was blowing her own head up being in this big mansion. It had her thinking she didn't need roscoe no more.

"Yo, you talking nutty right now. I don't know who you think you talking to. You damn sure ain't talking to 'Scoe like that."

"I'm talking to you. Who else would be talking too? I ain't fuckin with you." She stood her ground.

"You playin games? Bring yo ass home now. If you don't leave where ever the fuck you at right now, when you do come back, all your shit will be on the street along with your ass. In the rain."

"Roscoe why you gotta do this? You put your fuckin hands on me!" she whined.

She started getting soft thinking about all her possessions being outside along with being homeless. That immediately started fucking with her head and she sighed in desperation.

"I don't give a damn. Bring your ass home now. I'm not playing around." He hung up on her.

She closed her phone and stood still for a second, trying to hold back tears. She looked in the mirror at herself. Looking into her eyes they filled with water. Slowly the tears dripped down her cheeks. She examined her skin and the tone of it seemed to be uneven. Her eyes looked tired, with dark circles under them. She wasn't happy with who she saw staring back at her. The black eye liner on her eyes was smudge from her tears. She tore a piece of toilet paper off the roll and wiped under her eyes, wiped her nose and forced herself to stop crying. She pulled herself together and left the bathroom.

"Hey babe. I gotta go. I have something I need to take care of; last minute," she said to Kenny as she walked out the bathroom.

He looked disappointed as he stood up and walked towards her. "Everything ok?" he asked concerned. He walked up to her and placed his hands on her arms. His big hands warmed her and slightly calmed her.

"Yeah everything is fine but I have to go handle something," she replied.

She didn't want to leave but she knew she couldn't have Roscoe home alone, waiting and mad. It was time to handle the situation and that was to face him. He leaned down and began to kiss her on the neck in an attempt to get her to stay. She got weak in the knees at the touch of his lips instantly. They ran up and down her neck and then over to her lips. He sucked her bottom lip with a little pressure that made her want to jump on him that very second.

They continued to kiss passionately as he rubbed his hands down her arms, grabbing her hips and pulled her closer to his body. He wanted her badly and she felt the same way. For a moment she forgot all about Roscoe and got lost in lust. She ran her hands down his brown muscular arms and got even more excited. He bent down and grabbed her from her legs and picked her up. She wrapped both legs around his waist as he walked her up the stairs to his bedroom and they continued to kiss. He laid her down on his bed and she squirmed around a little.

He took off his black diamond necklace and his watch and placed it in the top drawer on his dresser. She wondered how much that type of jewelry cost. There was no doubt on the authenticity of the jewels so it amazed her that she was with someone with so much money to blow. The last time she saw him he had on a yellow diamond necklace. She smirked at the thought of who she was with.

On his way back over to the bed, he reached up and grabbed his t shirt and pulled it off. She admired his muscles and couldn't wait to run her hands over them some more. His chocolate skin was flawless and football did his body well. Within seconds he was pulling her clothes off and sliding inside her.

Immediately after, she scrambled herself together, throwing her clothes on. She fixed her hair in the mirror and started to put her shoes on. He sat up on the bed once he realized she was leaving. He thought his good loving was going to keep her around and have her forget all about whatever it was she needed to handle.

"You leaving?" he asked. Not used to a woman leaving right after sex unless he asked her to, it left him confused.

"Yeah babe, I told you that I had to take care of something. I will call you when I get home and done with everything."

She walked over and gave him a kiss on the lips. She met him at the restaurant and followed him to his house in her own car so she didn't need to rely on him for a ride back. He didn't even have time to put something on to walk her downstairs. She rushed her way out on her own and sped off to handle things with Roscoe.

She stood outside the apartment door, scared. She worried that he was going to hit her again and nervous that she wouldn't be able to stop him. After taking a few deep breaths, she placed her hand on the cold door knob and turned slowly. It was locked, so she reached in her purse and pulled out her keys. As soon as she started to put them in the hole, she heard Roscoe on the other end unlock it. He must have heard the jingle of the keys and the door swung open. Standing there stood an angry Roscoe with a look in his eye that could literally kill.

She took a few stumbled steps back, frightened by the door swinging open. She stared at him, unsure of what the next move should be. There was no need to make a move though because he immediately grabbed her by both arms, pulled her inside and shut the door. He threw her up against the wall with such force she banged the back of her head. Her first reaction was to scream. He placed one big hand over her mouth and leaned in close to her face. He placed all his weight on her body against the wall so she couldn't get away or even move. She was helpless and her mind raced, trying to figure out how to get away. Fear overcame her; fear for her life.

"Where were you at?" he questioned as he stared in her eyes angrily.

She didn't want to answer but she knew she had to. Trying to think of a lie she stood there silenced. He pushed his weigh up against her harder when she gave no response. He was going to find out where she had been if it took all night.

"I said where were you at?" he asked with a little more aggression.

Her mind was blank and she couldn't even think to answer him. She just wanted to get away, so she squirmed and squirmed to get free to not avail. He picked her up off the wall and threw her on the floor. He slung her body down like a rag doll and hovered over her. She inched away from him as he took steps following her; he continued to ask where she was and what she was doing. By this time Simone was hysterically crying and answering questions was not even an option. She could barely even breathe straight with all the sobs escaping her mouth.

"Answer me bitch!" he yelled down to her. She flinched at his outburst and decided to just tell him. It didn't seem that he was going to let up and she feared being hit.

"I was with my friend," she whimpered out.

"Your friend? Your friend?" He stood up straight. "Now you know I ain't dumb. This friend a man?" he yelled, placing an emphasis on the word friend.

She shook her head yes in shame and just as quickly as she nodded her head he leaned in and smacked her, right across the cheek. She grabbed her face, and curled up in a ball, expecting more blows. But none came; she peeked up and saw him pacing back and forth with his hands running over his head.

"So you come up in my place. Live in my house and go see some other man?" he asked and stopped pacing.

"I'm sorry. I was just hurt because you hit me," She lied; she would have went to see Kenny even if he didn't hit her.

"So you go see someone else? What the fuck do you think this is? A game? My feelings are a game to you?"

He picked her up off the ground and again threw her up against the wall. She closed her eyes and cried. He grabbed a handful of her hair from the top of her head. She couldn't believe what was going on.

"Who is it?" he asked.

She continued to cry and squeezed her eyes shut, just wanting to disappear from the situation. He continued to question who this friend was until she finally whispered out his name. He tightened the grip on her hair and wanted to know where he was from.

"You don't know him," she whimpered.

"How the fuck you know? Kenny from where!" he yelled in her face and gave her a punch to her lower stomach.

The pain shot through her body and instantly she knew something was really wrong. Her baby. The baby she didn't want to begin with and was planning on ridding herself of anyway. She wasn't far along and her heart was so cold at this point in her life that the acceptance that she most likely just lost her baby wasn't even a factor to her. The pain was unbearable and that's all she could think about, soon she felt a warm moisture began to leak down her thighs. Blood she thought.

"He plays football," she gave in and spilled the info.

"Football?" he questioned in a state of confusion as he let go of her hair.

"Yea, for the Giants," she reached up and ran her hands through her hair in an attempt to brush it off her face. She wiped the tears streaming down her cheeks and held onto her stomach.

"You fucking with some rich football player?" he questioned when he already knew the answer.

He was just shocked and didn't expect it. He thought it would be some local player around the way, stealing what was his. Now he was left standing dumbfounded and actually a little intimidated and jealous. Money was all he had to hold over her head. Money and place to stay was his bargaining chip. He knew Simone was down and out and he was taking advantage of the helpless state she was in. Now that he knew she was dealing with someone with way more money than him, it left him feeling small. He stepped back away from her.

"Is that who you want?" he asked.

She didn't know what to say because at that very moment she saw the vulnerability in him. She was trapped by his puppy dog eyes that quick. She didn't give him an answer and slid down the wall. Sitting on the floor she continued to cry, and wiped her nose and eyes on her sleeve. He said nothing more and went into the bedroom, slammed the door and locked it. She got up, laid on the couch, and cried to herself until she heard him snoring in the other room. She slowly crept into the bedroom and got a pair of sneakers, slid them on and left silently to the emergency room.

When she was released from the hospital she met up with a friend of hers from the club who let her stay at her apartment for a few nights until she could she could get the courage to return to Roscoe's apartment. After close to a week she finally went back and she quickly plugged her cell phone into the charger and powered it up. After grabbing some clothes and stuffing them in a bag, she ran to the bathroom and tried to brush her teeth as quickly as possible. With no idea when he left, or how long he would be gone, she rushed to get out before he came back.

Clueless to where she was going, she had her bag in her hands and cell phone in the other. She paced back in forth in front of the door trying to figure out what she should do. Leave or stay? The possibilities of each ran through her head and it left her confused. Without even a second more to think and make a decision, the front door swung open. Roscoe and his best friend, Gilly, walked in the apartment.

He noticed the bag in her hand immediately. "You ain't going nowhere."

He grabbed the bag out her hand and tossed it in the bedroom. She knew there was about to be some more drama and her stomach flipped upside down at the thought of what was about to happen next. She took a few steps back and Gilly flopped down on the couch like he was about to watch a show.

"How you doing Simone?" Gilly asked as he made himself comfortable in an uncomfortable situation.   She didn't bother answering and her eyes never even left Roscoe, burning a hole in his face; she starred.

"So you're going to take us to Kenny's house," Roscoe demanded as he pulled a chair up from the kitchen table and took a seat.

"What? For what?" Simone replied, hoping he didn't want to fight him.

He's a professional athlete and anything like this could ruin his career she thought. She never wanted things to turn out like this. Standing in the middle of the floor with both guys on opposite ends of her made her nervous so she inched her way back towards the bedroom.

"Because I said so. We gonna go handle business and you're going to show me where he lives. And you're not going to tell him."

"Come on Roscoe. I won't fuck with him no more. I will leave it alone! You don't gotta go over there. He didn't do nothing to you, he didn't even know about you," she pleaded with him to change his mind.

"We are going to rob him. I know you know where he keeps stuff at in his house," he informed her.

"I don't! I've only been there once; I don't even remember how to get there," she lied.

She knew exactly how to get there and matter of fact it was still in her GPS. If her memory served her right, she also knew exactly where he kept his jewelry. In the top drawer in his bedroom, she saw him place it in there before sex. Assuming that there were more in there that would be exactly the spot they needed to hit.

"You going to tell me you don't remember where this man lives? Are you fuckin' serious? Do I look like a dumb ass to you?" he yelled as he got angry and stood up.

'Aw hell' she thought to herself. She knew it was about to be a problem.

"Is that what you're telling me? You don't know where he lives or where he keeps his money?" He got closer to her and she took a step back.

"No 'scoe, I don't know!" again she lied to him.

He knew she was lying and if he didn't know for sure he was going to assume she was lying. He was the furthest person from rational and his temper compared to none. Simone knew of his crazy ways but never knew to the extent because she rushed right into the relationship with him. It scared her because she knew she didn't really have any options but to beg Isis or Chantel for a place to stay which really weren't options for her. She hated to be needy and look helpless to them. They both intimidated her and no way did she want to give them any more reason to have control over her.

Not happy with her answer, he quickly got up close to her and grabbed her by the neck again. The fact that Gilly was in the room didn't even seem to faze him and neither did it faze Gilly. They must have both been used to violence and abuse to women as it seemed like a normal thing taking place.

"Do you know where Kenny lives?" he asked again, while he held one hand firmly around her throat. She tried unsuccessfully to claw it away with both hands. She shook her head no because again she couldn't get the word out.

He loosened up his grip and back hand smacked her across the face. She flung down to the ground and cried out. She couldn't believe this was happening again and more importantly while Gilly sat there like nothing was happening.

"Since you don't know how to answer me right, we gon' have to do this the hard way. Get the fuck up Simone!" he shouted at her.

She cradled her head in her arms and rocked back and forth on the floor crying. She took a second to look through her arms and saw Gilly sitting back on the couch with a smirk on his face. He must have been enjoying this. '*Triflen ass bastard*' she thought to herself. She didn't move when he told her to, she was paralyzed with fear. Out of the cracks between her two arms she peeked up nervously and saw Roscoe coming closer, so she braced herself for another blow. Instead he grabbed her by the arm and pulled her up and shoved her towards the bedroom.

"Go in the room," he demanded.

She took a few slow steps and he shoved her to speed her pace up. Once inside the room, he shut the door and pushed her onto their bed that they once shared in affection. He grabbed her face and shoved his tongue down her throat as she tried to move away. His power over her was a turn on to him. He was always excited by power always, whether it was over a women or man. He enjoyed having control over everyone in any situation. Breaking her mouth free of his, she used both hands to push his face back.

"Roscoe! Stop!" she shouted and squirmed around trying to get loose from under his body that leaned on top of her.

Of course she was not successful; because he was much heavier then she couldn't move. He grabbed her by the arms and turned her around on the bed. Her face was smashed into the blanket and she could hardly breathe, forcing her to turn her face sideways to get air. Roughly he yanked at her grey sweat pants and pale pink underwear.

She couldn't believe what was happening and how he could think about sex at a time like this. She felt silly, bare, and helpless. Out of breath and energy she stopped struggling. After a brief second of her not moving, she realized he let his grip of her go so she turned back to face him. He quickly smacked her across the face, forcing her to lie face back down on the bed. Her legs dangled off the end and he pulled her by the hips. Now her ass was directly in his crotch and she knew what was about to happen.

"You going to take me to Kenny house tomorrow?" he asked calmly.

"I told you I can't do that. I don't know where he lives," she continued to lie in fear of Kenny's safety and at this point she still didn't know what Roscoe was capable of.

That was the last time he was going to ask and get the wrong answer. He grabbed a handful of her long silky hair and wrapped his hand around it and he tugged back. Her neck was strained backwards and she was struggling to breathe in and out.

"So you want to play games then huh?" he asked as he undid his belt buckle with his free hand.

The only thing that came out her mouth was gasp for air. Her head was pulled back so far it was making it difficult for her to breathe properly. In a matter of seconds he was stroking his thick brown penis as it grew longer and thicker. Once he was hard, he shoved it inside her two lips and pounded her out as she painfully yelled for him to stop. He was not being mindful of her at all and manically pounded harder and harder.

"You still not gonna take me to his house?" he grunted out.

"I....can't," she managed to cry out.

Still unsatisfied with her answer, he pulled out, spit on his hand and applied it to his penis. Without warning he began to shove it in her ass. She screamed out in pain and tried to squirm away but wasn't getting very far. He tugged on her hair each time she tried to get away. Inch by inch he entered her as tears streamed down her face. Never before had she had anal sex and without her consent made it even worse. Half way in he stopped.

"You know where he lives?" he asked again.

For fear of him ripping her, she gave in finally. "I do," she confessed, trying desperately to relax her muscles.

"So you was lying to me huh?" he continued to shove inside her until he could pump in and out. Her screams grew more and more intense as he began a continuous motion in and out of her exit only hole.

"Please...stop....your hurting me," she screamed out.

"You know where his stuff at?" he asked and tugged her hair.

"Yes...Yes!!" she yelled throwing up the white flag, giving up completely.

As soon as he was out of her she climb completely on the bed and curled herself into a ball, still crying. She was in so much pain and embarrassment. He stood, staring down at her, while he continued to stroke his penis. Clearly he wasn't finished and wanted to release before this episode was over. She feared he would come back for more, so she balled herself up as tight as she could and scouted to the back of the bed. There was nowhere for her to go.

He sucked his teeth at the sight of her and pulled his pants up, knowing he gave her enough pain he decided to leave her alone for now. The plan was set in motion and tomorrow while Kenny went out of town for his game, they would be robbing him naked of every quality possession in his house. The thought of it made him smirk as he left the bedroom and shut the door. Gilly and he headed out for the night to get themselves into some NYC trouble, leaving Simone there hurt, crying and scared.

14

~ Robbery 101 ~

The thought ran through her head about ten more times within the last few seconds. Should she warn Kenny? Would Roscoe find out? She sat nervously tapping her foot on the floor. Her eyes were glued to her cell phone that she gripped tightly in her sweaty hand. Her nerves were all over the place as she waited for the second Roscoe would walk in the door. After glancing at the clock a few times she decided that he was probably still at the club and wouldn't be home for at least another hour. After the phone rang with no answer on Kenny's side, she left a message telling him not to call her back, it's important but don't call back and to just read the text message. Immediately when she hung up she began texting him an explanation. She let him in on Roscoe's plans tomorrow that he and his boy would be trying to rob his house. She explained that she had nothing to do with it and that she is trying her best to stop it from happening. It saddened her because she knew this would be the end of her relationship with him because all of this is just unnecessary drama she is bringing into his life.

To make sure Roscoe knew nothing of that text, she deleted the messages after she sent it and her call log in her phone. There was no telling if he would go through her phone or not. She laid in bed, thinking, praying, and hoping that tomorrow wouldn't turn out the way he planned it.

Thoughts of her mom and dad somehow began to run through her head. The communication between them was almost nonexistent. Her dad pretty much fell off the face of the earth with working on his new business and new girlfriend. The last time they spoke, he called to tell her they got engaged. It almost made her want to vomit right on the phone. The once perfect relationship she had with her dad was broke so suddenly. He turned out to be just as terrible as her mother always said he was. Since her mother came clean and expressed how she felt for the first time, they still haven't spoke. Each one of them harboring guilt and resentment, made it hard for them to out their pride aside.

Simone sat wondering how her life would have been if she listened to her mom and went away to college. Would she have been in college, sitting pretty with a nice bank account supplied by her mom? Driving around campus in the newest BMW, carrying the latest LV purse, and never having to worry about what man she was going to scheme to get a bill paid. Would she be able to focus on school and making something out of herself instead of taking shot after shot to go in the club and slide up and down a pole so she could feed herself and pay rent. The possibilities ran through her head, just giving her heartache and a headache. She tried to push her parents out her mind, but it wasn't working.

In deep thought, she let the next hour and a half pass before she finally started to drift off into sleep. As soon as her eyes began to close, she was awakened by the front door swinging open. In walked a drunken Roscoe and Gilly. Her heart dropped into her stomach as she watched the two of them from her bedroom, as they came inside and stumbled around talking loudly. She hoped the worse of the night had already occurred and that they would leave her alone. To no avail, they both walked into the bedroom.

"You still up?" Roscoe slurred.

"Yea," she answered, already annoyed but she tried to hide it.

"Gilly sleepin on the couch so don't be walking around showing your ass," he said.

Gilly chuckled and walked back to the living room and fell onto the couch. It wasn't long before he slid his sneakers off and made himself comfortable. In a matter of seconds he was knocked out.

"Ok baby," she answered while she tried to put on a pleasant front.

All the while she was scheming a way out of this situation. Her mind could only think of Isis or Chantel as help. Would they let her stay with them, and would she even be safe there? All of that thinking wasn't doing her any good at the present time. She was stuck in the apartment with Roscoe for the night at least.

He undressed down to his boxers and shut the bedroom door. Once in bed he began to rub his hands along Simone's curvy hips and she prayed that he would just leave her alone. She didn't want to be touched or bothered by him. Sex would definitely be a chore tonight because in no way was she interested in doing it. She knew if she resisted it would just be more hits and pain. His hand slowly began to stop rubbing her and she noticed his heavy breathing. He fell asleep; the alcohol and soft, warm bed knocked him out. She fell into a deep sleep herself, exhausted from the day's events.

When she woke, Roscoe was still sleep and Gilly was gone. She lifted herself up over Roscoe without touching him and careful not to move the bed. The longer he slept the better off she would be she thought. Once in the kitchen, she pulled the cabinets open, one by one and found nothing at all to eat. Last she looked in the refrigerator and again saw nothing. She realized she hasn't eaten anything since her early dinner last night. The sounds of her stomach got louder and the headache from last night's drama got worse. She needed food and needed it now.

Her appearance was nowhere near suitable to go out to any store so she had to get herself together first. She quickly hopped in the shower after she peeled her night clothes off, leaving them on the floor. When she stepped out, she quietly crept back into the bedroom to find clothes to put on. Once dressed, she grabbed her toothbrush and toothpaste and headed back to the bathroom. She took her right hand and wiped the steam from the mirror so she could look at herself. Stunned froze by the image that stared back at her, she leaned in closer to get a better look.

Her left eye was puffy from her cheekbone to under her eye, and a purple tint began to surface. A crack in her bottom lip revealed a small amount of dried blood and lastly, a small whelp ran down the side of her neck to her shoulder. She didn't even realize she was cut and bruised up because her mind was just too many places at once. She stared at her face, disgusted at the reflection, inside and out.

Her hands gripped the ledge of the sink and her fingers dug in until she felt an unbearable pain. She reached her right up hand up, balled it into a fist and pounded on the wall in anger. The mirror clattered lightly as the pressure from her fist landed on the wall. She began to cry hysterically. Uncontrollably she let tears run down her face and howls out her mouth as she fell to the ground in a ball. She squeezed her eyes closed as her head started to hurt and her teeth clenched shut. 'God please help me' she whispered to herself repeatedly and rocked back and forth.

"What you crying for?" Roscoe walked in the bathroom, squinting his eyes from the light. He leaned on the doorframe, looking down at her.

The whimpering stopped and she quickly jumped up. Embarrassed that she woke him with her cries, she wiped her tears away. The way he made her feel over the past few days was nothing but terrified. Her eyes couldn't even look at his, her gazed stayed low.

"Nothing," she replied softly.

The redness of her face caught his attention and he noticed how puffy it was. Although he hit her with no remorse, he began to feel bad that her face bared the scars of his angry rage. She grabbed her toothbrush and toothpaste and turned the faucet on. He slid up behind her, wrapping his arms her waist.

He leaned in close to her ear, "Baby I know I overreacted. I didn't mean to hurt you last night."

Her stomach and she wanted to vomit at the touch of his hands and the sound of his voice. She struggled to keep a straight face because he could see her in the mirror. After a brief moment, he returned the bedroom and didn't bother taking a shower; he just picked up a pair of blue jeans and pulled them on and put on a black thermal shirt. After sitting on the edge of the bed, he pulled his Timbs on and tied them. His plot to rob Kenny was really the only thing on his mind. Imagining the jewels and cash that he had lying around that big mansion of his, flash through his mind. Even though realistically most people don't leave stashes of cash in their house, Roscoe wasn't thinking straight. He just wanted to get in there and see what he could get his hands on. Intelligence wasn't Roscoe's strong suite. He was a shoot first and ask questions later type of man.

"Hurry up and get yourself together. We heading to Kenny's crib when Gilly gets here," he yelled into the bathroom.

Simone's stomach sunk and she froze listening to Roscoe talk. The words stung her like a bee even though she knew that was the plan. It just got real.

"Ok," she replied barely audible due to the toothpaste still in her mouth.

She purposely took her time to get finished because she wanted to avoid going at all cost. Once Gilly arrived, she knew it was nothing else she could do. Leaving it in fate's hands she decided that she had no choice. She mopped out the bathroom and dug in the closet for a hoody. She pulled the hood over her head and insecurely tried to cover her battered face as much as possible. On the way out the door, she grabbed a pair of sunglasses and threw them on.

Silent the whole way to Kenny's house, Simone clenched her teeth. Her nerves were getting to her and she felt horrible for directing them to his house. As they pulled up on his street, she pointed the house out. They drove past it up a few houses and pulled over on the street. They didn't want to pull up in his long driveway in fear for someone noticing the car. They walked up the side of the house behind the shrubs to the back door. Gilly was a master thief so getting inside was nothing but a routine job for them. He disarmed the house and picked the lock with ease.

Once inside, Simone stood still near the door. She didn't want to go any further or touch anything. She watched enough criminal and court shows to know that all they needed was a strand of hair to convict you with DNA. Gilly and Roscoe wore black gloves to trap their fingerprints and started going through every door, drawer, closet or space they could invade. They told Simone she didn't need gloves since she had already been to his house previously. After going through the whole downstairs area they realized there wasn't any cash lying around so they started stacking up electronics he had near the door. They knew they could sell this stuff and make some good change.

"Get a trash bag and put that small stuff in it," Roscoe instructed Simone.

"I didn't say I was helping. I just told you how to get here," Simone snapped back.

"I don't give a fuck what you said. Pack that shit up," he demanded.

She knew if she didn't then it would just mean more problems for her so she rolled her eyes and began looking in the kitchen cabinets for a bag. She nervously looked around expecting Kenny or some police officers to jump out any second but nothing happened. After coming up with nothing but a shopping bag, she threw the small things in like his iPod, one of his phones, and his game systems they had found in the family room. She chuckled to herself at the lack of stuff they were coming up with and wondered if Kenny had ever got her message or not. Certainly if he did then they would have stopped what was going on so she began to think he never got it. At that moment she thought to check the phone she just threw in the bag. It was locked and she didn't know the code. The only thing she could see was that there were missed calls and text messages. Her stomach sank when she realized that he probably never got the message because this was the phone it probably went to.

"Roscoe come on let's go! What's taking so long?" she whined in an attempt to hurry the job. She wanted out.

The kitchen led to the living room and family room where they were unplugging the sound system that was connected to the flat screen. *'Just steal the whole damn house'* she thought to herself. She couldn't believe that she was involved in something like this. After they got the sound system out, they made their way upstairs. She dreaded what they would find in his bedroom. Her mind flashed back to his top drawer where he placed his jewelry the night she was with him. She prayed that he would have been smart enough to put it somewhere safe while he was away. In that very moment she was sure that he didn't. She began walking up the stairs and heard Gille say "jackpot." She rolled her eyes and went to see what was found.

Gillie stood over Kenny's dresser pulling out a black diamond necklace and a huge iced out watch. He looked them over and kept digging in the drawer; pulled out some loose cash and a second yellow diamond chain. A wide grin crossed his face as he stuffed it all in his pockets and began opening up the lower drawers, hoping to find more.

"Yo, Gillie come see this shit," Roscoe yelled from the other room.

Simone and Gillie both went into the walk in closet that looked like it was just a sneaker room to see what Roscoe was talking about. Their eyes were immediately drawn to the stacks of green cash that Roscoe was pulling out of a shoe box that was stacked on one of the shelves next to some sneakers. Simone shook her head at Kenny's stupidity and lack of a safe like most rich people would have in their house.

"Yo dawg! Look at this shit. It's all hundreds," Roscoe said as he started to put the money back in the box.

Gillie walked over, looked at the money and began checking every other shoe box in the room but only came up with more sneakers. Roscoe grabbed the box and ran out to the hallway. He thought for a second if he should continue to look around for anything more or take what he got. He decided not to be greedy and take what they got. He knew they hit the jackpot with that shoe box of cash.

"Let's get outta here," Roscoe directed and headed down the stairs with Simone and Gillie following snatching a few Gucci belts out the closet.

Roscoe was stopped dead in his tracks at the bottom of the steps and stared into the eyes of a woman walking in the front door. A young twenty something year old woman stood there holding her LV purse and removed her sunglasses. Simone knew it had to be a girlfriend or a woman friend he was dealing with. She had the key to his house and she was young and beautiful. The look on her face was nothing short of terrified. She looked like she had seen a ghost. They stood still and silent for a few seconds before Roscoe came up with what he thought was a good plan.

"Oh hey. I didn't know Kenny was having company," Roscoe said to the girl.

"Well me either. I didn't see a car out front," she answered confused.

Her eyes darted to each of their faces, trying to read the situation. Her next reaction was to reach in her purse and place her hand on her mace. She didn't pull it out yet because she wasn't sure if these were friends of Kenny's or not.

"Yeah it's on the street. I just came to pick something up; he left the back door open for me," Roscoe replied.

"Why would he leave the back door open? He wouldn't do something like that."

"Well ask him then. I'm out," Roscoe said, trying to take control of the situation.

The three of them walked past her and out the front door, leaving behind all the electronics they compiled near the back door. She immediately pulled out her cell phone to contact Kenny and find out if these were his friends. By the time she hung up with him and called the police, the three of them made it to their car and were out of sight.

Simone nervously tapped her foot in the car as she thought about how they got caught. She knew the girl didn't buy their story and they left all the packed up stuff near the back door with her finger prints all on it. She knew it was over for her. They only made it out with the shoe box of money and the jewelry from his top drawer.

As soon as they returned back to Roscoe's apartment they began to count the money in the shoe box. Simone was too on edge to even sit down or relax. She paced back and forth as her mind filled with a million and one what ifs. There was no way that the amount of money they stole was going to be able to get them away from getting caught. It was a nice amount of money but really wasn't anything significant. It's not like they could just up and leave to another country. She knew Roscoe's hood ass didn't even have a passport and neither did she. They quickly counted the stacks of hundreds that were packed in the box and talked about what they would do with the money. It was a little over 70k in the box and Roscoe and Gillie were going to split it. Simone of course was not included in the cut.

Gillie pulled out the jewels from his pocket and showed them to Roscoe. Gillie knew exactly where to take the stuff to get cash for them and he was positive he would get at least fifteen-thousand for all three pieces. Simone rolled her eyes at how dumb Kenny was to have that type of cash sitting around in his house. She defiantly didn't expect that.

After the cash was split down the middle, Gillie headed out to see about the jewels. Simone was on constant edge even after Roscoe told her to relax plenty of times. She still walked around the apartment with her nerves jumping. Her sneakers still on and her brain constantly working. She was thinking of a way out and her first order of business was to get her things and get out of Roscoe's apartment.

The second Roscoe stepped out the apartment, Simone started to pack an overnight bag. Momentarily she began to worry that if she left she wouldn't be able to come back and get the rest of her stuff so she began to pack it all up. Everything she owned she stuffed in suitcases, duffle bags, trash bags and boxes. She called Chantel and frantically told her to please pick her up it was an emergency and to bring Trey's truck. She explained that she needed to stay with her for a few days. Her plan wasn't well thought out and she knew that Roscoe could find her there or at work at the club. All she knew was she that at that very moment she wanted to get her and her stuff out his apartment.

Once Trey pulled up with Chantel, she asked them to help her get her stuff. They quickly packed her stuff up in his truck and headed back to Simone's place. Once they saw the bruises on her face they didn't even need to ask what was wrong. Trey told her that if she needed any help that she could always call him and since she was friends with Chantel, he would protect her as family. She really appreciated it and for once felt that she was with people who genuinely care for her.   She took in the moment and felt safe and loved yet still helpless.

Once they unpacked everything into Chantel's apartment, Simone began telling her exactly what happened.   Being careful not to leave any details out, she told her step by step about the abuse, to the text and call to Kenny, to the robbery.   She desperately needed advice and Chantel seemed to always know what to do.

"I can't even believe that! You know your finger prints will be all over that stuff by the door. You shouldn't have touched anything!" Chantel exclaimed as she jumped up from the couch.

Her mind was racing for a solution because she wanted to help Simone badly.   The outcome of this could only be bad and she really wanted Simone to get her life together. This whole situation was no help to that.

"I know. I had no choice," she replied and sucked her teeth. "Oh shit!" Simone screamed and jumped up. "Oh my God! The cell phone is still at his house in that bag! The phone with the message I sent!"

Chantel stood still confused, thinking exactly what that cell phone would mean to the situation, "What's so significant about the phone?"

"I mean if they read that message they will know that I didn't want to do it and that it wasn't my plan," Simone explained.

Chantel stood staring at her, "Girl please. The police don't care if you wanted to do it or not because you still did it. Now when Kenny or the police read the message they don't even have to bother doing finger prints. They can come straight for you. Either way you're involved." Chantel popped Simone's bubble.

She didn't want to seem hopeless but she didn't want Simone to be naïve about things either. "What about turning yourself in?" she added.

"Hell no! I'm not going to the police!" Simone declined.

"Look, you don't really have much of an option. They know you're involved. So you can turn yourself in and tell your side of the story willingly, get bailed out if they do lock you up, get a lawyer and I'm sure you can beat it. Or you can have them come look for you, force a guilty statement, snitch on Roscoe and Gille and get locked up."

Simone sat thinking about the possibilities and knew neither one sounded good. She knew Chantel was right though but she didn't want to have to deal with it. She wished it could all just disappear but she was learning more and more that life is only what you make it and you can't erase what you did. Finally she made the decision that she would go turn herself in but first there were some things she needed to take care of.

"You should speak to a lawyer before you go. That way they can tell you the best thing to do and if they do lock you up, you will already have a lawyer that knows your case and have you out asap," Chantel said.

She felt bad for her friend but knew she fucked up. 70 thousand dollars was a lot to steal from someone's house, along with his jewelry. She knew there was no easy way out of this.

"Yo to be honest I can't afford a lawyer," Simone said and hung her head low.

"What? You ain't got no money? You swing on a pole every night; you mean to tell me you don't have anything saved up? I thought you were making good money there!" Chantel questioned.

Chantel was shocked. How can you be degrading your body every night but still broke she thought to herself, defeats the whole purpose of it.

"You're walking around with a thirteen-hundred dollar Louis Vuitton purse on your arm and you can't afford a lawyer?" she added.

Chantel knew she had completely failed in teaching her girl any type of street smarts. Simone was more lost then she ever imagined. Money rules the world and if you aren't getting it, stacking it, and saving it, then you are a fool to be spending it. Simone failed to realize that half these people that were getting money were spending it as soon as they got it. They weren't smart enough to make sure that when the supply of easy money stopped they were still able to live like it never did. That was Chantel and Trey's goal and she thought that anyone would try to live by that rule as well. Too bad Simone was just clueless and needed someone to hold her hand through life.

"I don't have it. I've been really low on money lately. I can hardly pay my bills," she admitted.

Simone felt terrible and useless. She didn't want to ask Chantel for money and there was no time to go make some quick cash. Once again her mind raced and she wanted a drink or some drugs. She needed something because she was driving herself crazy.

"So what about your homegirl Isis? That's your friend right. She chillin in that big ass mansion you told me about and driving a Benz. I know she got money to spare," Chantel suggested.

Simone was silent. She knew that she and Isis weren't on the best page lately and she hasn't heard from her for a while. "I don't even know where she been at. I think she mad at me or something."

"Are you kidding me? You tried to whoop my ass over her and you can't even go to her for help when you down and out," Chantel inquired and almost wanted to laugh at her.

"I know," Simone answered embarrassed.

"Well I do know one other option," Chantel began to suggest, "You could always call your parents."

"Oh hell no. You already know they wouldn't help me! If they would then I would have been called them for help with shit," Simone whined.

"No there is a difference with asking for help with bills and bullshit than asking for help to keep your ass out of jail," Chantel interjected. Simone sat silent.

"Alright look I will pay for your lawyer but you have got to find a way to pay me back when this is all over. I'm serious. I want every penny back. So do what you gotta do." Chantel said realizing she was going to have to dip in her stash of money that her brother had left her.

That stash was for emergencies only and this was an emergency. She hated that she had to use some of it but she knew it was something she had to do. Even though Simone had pissed her off and she tried over and over to help her, she knew she couldn't turn her back on her friend. Chantel was raised as a loyal person and she would never lose that trait.

Chantel immediately got on the phone with a couple lawyers and scheduled to go see some for free consultations. After the two girls visited three lawyers, they picked one that they believed would be the best for them. His name was Mr. Goldstien, a middle aged white man who knew every trick in the book. He had been practicing law for years and had a great track record for winning. He also seemed to be sympathetic to blacks who were led astray. He had deep inner drive to help less fortunate or under privileged people rise above their obstacles faced by them in society. Not many times did Simone meet someone like this in her life but now was one time she was glad to shake the hand of a helpful white man.

The two girls came in dressed like sultry young sex pots, hoping that their good looks would get them a better deal on the rate. What they didn't know was that he saw right through the low cut shirts, and tight pants. He saw two girls screaming out for help. In no way did he want to take advantage of them as most men they met in their life did.

He offered the girls his lowest rate that he could. He was positive he would be able to keep her out with her confession, giving up Roscoe and Gillie, and the fact that she did not have any of the money or jewelry on her. He knew that she shouldn't have a problem with this especially with his representation.

After sitting in his luxurious office for a few hours, they finally ended the meeting. Next step was for Simone to go talk to the detectives at the police station. Mr. Goldstein already made a call to the station to alert them that she would be on her way. Before Simone could even make it out the building she had to run to the bathroom and throw up. Assuming it was just nerves, Chantel cleaned her up and gave her a hug. She held her hand all the way to the station that coincidentally was only a few blocks away.

Simone held tightly onto Chantel for their last hug. They two didn't want to let go. They finally let go and Simone could feel the tears beginning to well up in the corners of her eyes. Chantel hated to see her go through this.

"Don't even cry. Girl, just do what you have to do. Tell the truth and you should be fine. You let them know your life was threatened and don't you dare be afraid to let them know where Roscoe lives and that he has the money!"

She took a step back from Simone, "You got a great lawyer. He seems to know what he is talking about and he said you should be ok.'"

Mr. Goldstein and Simone finally walked up the steps of the police station after a tearful goodbye between the two girls. Chantel couldn't help but feel terrible for what Simone was going through but at the same time she missed Trey so bad. She couldn't wait to get back to him, the past twenty-four hours she had been dealing with Simone and her situation that she has totally been abandoning her man. She called him as soon as she turned to walk away. Hearing his voice would make her feel one-hundred percent better.

"Baby girl! It's official!" Trey shouted into the phone as he picked up her call.

"What's going on?" Chantel asked in confusion. "What's official?"

"Keys signed the contract with Def Jam baby! Its official! And I'm going to get some production on the album! They liked 8 of the tracks we already had so they just need a few more to finish the album and they are gonna put him out. They are really excited about him so it's going to happen fast!"

"That's great! Oh my God baby! I'm so happy for you!" Chantel replied.

Genuinely in a better mood now that she spoke to her man and heard the good news, they decided to go out and celebrate. First dinner and drinks and then they hit the club with Keys and his girlfriend. After drinking, dancing and more drinking they all headed home to call it a night. They still could believe the success they were finally achieving and in a legal way. Keys got his nick name from the drug trade. It was no coincidence his raw street credibility was in his favor when in pursue of the record deal. Def Jam executives could sense his realness and knew this was a marketing jackpot!

Keys and Trey have been good friends for several years and long wanted to get out the drug trade and this was finally their chance. They both decided to dedicate their full potential and time to this music business now. The drugs were going to be a thing of their past. Chantel couldn't be any happier! Even though she knew it would mean some financial changes for the short term, she also knew that in due time that the money would be coming back in again and legally this time. New beginnings she thought.

Once they returned home, the liquor had put them both to sleep almost immediately once they touched their bed. They woke the next morning, fully clothed still and both suffering hangover headaches. Once she came to her senses and sat up, she called to check on Simone. She didn't think about her all night and really spent her time enjoying her man's success so she was anxious and worried to find out what happened with her girl.

"Girl turn the news on!" Simone shouted into the phone as she answered it. "They arrested Gillie and Roscoe!"

Chantel reached over Trey's still sleep body and grabbed the remote control. "Which channel?"

"NBC. I think it's six," Simone replied. "They believed my story and with my lawyer there to bargain with them, they didn't arrest me. I was shitting bricks girl. I was so scared."

Chantel caught the very end of the story as the news flashed two mug shots of the two robbers and then a clip of Kenny playing football. "The police did recover the seventy-thousand dollars in missing cash but they are still searching for the missing jewelry. Kenny is extremely happy that someone came forward with information that led to the arrest." The news anchor finished the story off.

"Wow. I still can't even believe that. So you're off the hook? No problems?" Chantel questioned.

"Yeah I'm good. They didn't doubt anything I said really. They saw the bruises on my body, my eyes still swollen. They even asked did I want to press charges on Roscoe for assault as well. I just left it alone. I just want to be done with him. I'm so relieved," Simone explained and continued to watch the news. "Plus Roscoe has so many priors that they were looking for his third strike."

15

~ Survival of the Fittest ~

Meanwhile

"This is some muthafuckin bullshit," Isis mumbled under her breath.

She checked the time on her cell phone again as she paced back and forth around the corner. Getting anxious and growing tired of waiting; she began to walk back to her car. Her annoyance level was on ten and she began to think that someone set her up with an unreliable source. One of her dancer friends gave her the contact to someone who pushed pills. The person she used to get stuff from had mysteriously up and disappeared. She didn't question it too much and assumed he got himself caught up. On to the next she thought. This dealer allegedly had a lot more of a variety also if she ever decided to dabble in anything different which she planned on doing today. Oxycotin was on the order.

"Yo shorty," a tall, skinny light skin boy emerged from around the corner. "My bad I'm late. I got that good good though."

Isis rolled her eyes at him and pulled her purse around and dug inside, pulling out a little bag that she had the money in. "You got everything I asked for?"

"Yeah I got that. That is what I do baby girl," he answered and pulled out a little pouch of pills and handed them to her. She gave him the bag of money.

"Thanks. I'll call you again sometime soon."

She turned to leave and instantly regretted the transaction. Three uniformed police officers began walking towards her. She turned around and saw the tall lanky boy walking off with two men in suits. A setup, she thought. Not knowing what to do next, she stood still waiting for them to approach; there was no time to run. She was caught and nothing she could do would get her out of this bind.

After being handcuffed and placed in the backseat of the car, her mind raced as she thought about what just happened and what was going to happen next. She fought the tears because she thought she was too tough to cry. Even alone her exterior shell was just as hard as her interior. Just then she caught the passenger officer's eyes in the mirror and a light bulb went off in her head.

"Yall really don't have to book me do you? No one would know if you just let me go," she pleaded. The passenger officer smirked but said nothing.

"Come on. I can't go to jail! I'm too pretty to go to jail."

"Your also to pretty to be buying illegal prescription pills," the driver officer replied.

"I got bills to pay that's all. I won't ever do it again, just let me go. I can do something for yall. Both of yall. You will like it, trust," She begged getting desperate. At this point she would do any and everything to not go to jail.

The officers looked at each other. Tempted by her offer and crooked as can be, they knew what they wanted. There was a silent exchange of agreement between the two of them. The only problem was that they had to book her because there was a good chance the detectives would find out if they didn't. They used a mole to set her up so there were probably reports written up on the case. Her charge was minor and usually the officers would have let a girl go in exchange for some sexual favors from someone as beautiful as Isis.

The driving officer was the one in charge and the passenger was a rookie. He took orders from the driver and trusted his judgment so when he pulled over on an alley way corner he knew that he had made the decision to take Isis up on the offer. He followed suit.

"What about Detective Santos?" the passenger officer asked.

"Don't worry about that young boy. I've been doing this for years and Santo's been working above me for years. I got this."

He turned back and looked at Isis who was tucked back in her seat looking around out the window. She noticed they stopped and knew what that meant. She got sick to her stomach at the thought of what was about to go down but she knew she had to do what she had to do.

"So what can you do for us?" the driver officer asked.

"Whatever you need," she replied ready to get dirty.

She took turns sucking both officers off expecting to go free but was disappointed greatly when they left the cuffs on her and forced her back in the car. They played her and she spent the next fifteen minutes screaming about how she was going to report them for rape. They laughed at her and knew no one would believe her or take her serious. They spent the car ride down taunting, teasing and humiliating her.

Once she got to the station, Detective Santos ran her information. He was pleasantly surprised when he realized they had just put out a warrant for her arrest on other chargers related to her "dating" business that they knew was really a sex for sale business. One of her bitter and angry workers, Nadine, snitched on the whole scheme. They set one of her girls up with an undercover cop and had been watching closely to her operation. The girl that AJ sent out on the date made it very obvious that she expected to be paid for sex. Once in the hotel room, the girl accepted the money and began to do her part when the police busted into the room. Isis was the newest and youngest madam in NYC and soon it would be all over the news. Her client list ran long and included some prominent figures in the city. This was a big bust for them and they were proudly taking her down.

She grabbed the phone and dialed AJ. It rang and rang with no answer. She tried again and still no answer. 'Where the fuck is he,' she thought to herself. Other then AJ she really had no one else to call. She didn't have a lawyer or any family. Her next try was Simone.

"Hey it's Isis. I need your help. The cops picked me up," Isis blurted into the phone when she picked up.

"Oh yeah? I heard. I'm watching the news. AJ too. Both of yall can suck my dick. Bitch!" Simone screamed into the phone and ended the call.

Isis sat dumbfounded with the phone in her hand. She didn't even understand what just happened or why. Once the Detective Santos explained to her that she had other charges and what they were, she started to make sense of it. She needed to get a lawyer and get one quick.

Simone couldn't believe what she was seeing on the news. They walked AJ into the police station in cuffs and didn't fail to mention his partner Isis who was already apprehended. She sat with her mouth wide open in shock as what she heard on the news confirmed what Chantel was trying to tell her all along. She was running an escort service and she was trying to reel her in slowly. They mentioned the website on the news also, stating that it had videos and images of women in sexual acts without their consent.

"Yo I can't even believe this. You was so right girl. I'm so sorry for not listening to you," Simone said into the phone.

She was still on the line with Chantel when Isis called from jail. She clicked over and quickly shut her down without even hesitating.

"Yeah girl. I tried to tell you. It's all good. Now you know what it is and you can move on. Look I'm about to leave Trey's now and head home. You there now right?"

"Yup I'm here and will be here when you get in. See ya."

The two girls decided to take the day and spend it together. They were working on repairing their tattered friendship and so far off to a good start. No Isis in the picture really eased both of their minds. She was a weight that just brought them down even though Simone didn't want to see it. Simone silently wondered how long she would be in jail for. She felt bad for her in a way. Without Isis and Roscoe around, Chantel felt that she could really work on getting Simone together. It just seemed like everything worked out for the best.

After a long day of shopping and lunch, they decided to catch a movie and then have a few drinks at a lounge. By the time they got out the movie Simone was in need of drinks. Simone had become quite the drinker and smoker over time. She actually had become a user of a lot more drugs but tried to keep it away from Chantel. They walked towards the subway so they could go downtown to a spot they knew was low key and relaxing yet still brought a good crowd of people to mingle with.

As they turned the corner towards the subway a van pulled up beside them. Out jumped four people dressed in all black with ski mask on. The two girls started to turn to run but got nowhere fast. The men grabbed them, covered their mouths and dragged them into the van. They kicked, screamed and tried to get free as much as possible until inside the van one of the men pulled out a gun.

"If yall don't shut the fuck up, I'm going to kill you both right here," the masked gunman said, waving the gun back and forth between Simone and Chantel.

They silenced their yelling and stopped their struggling. They both silently; prayed and begged God for his help. Neither one of them spent much time ever talking to God before but in a time of dire desperate need that was their instinct reaction. Simone began to cry and Chantel looked her in the eyes and wanted to reassure things would be ok, but she couldn't. She instead simply mouthed 'I love you.'

From that moment on their vision was blackened. They were blinded folded, hands tied behind their back and mouths gagged. They couldn't see where they were going and couldn't tell once they got there if they were even together anymore. They relied heavily on their other senses to touch and hear their surroundings. They both figured out that they were still together and placed on a cold floor. It felt like cement.

After what seemed liked hours of silence, the girls continued to lean up against each other. Suddenly a voice was heard and the girls became alert once again. Heart rate picking back up, palms getting sweaty again, the girls had no idea what to expect. They heard two voices speaking to each other in a nearby room but couldn't make out what they were saying. It was muffled by the walls.

Chantel's mind raced as she tried to figure out what was going on. Why would someone do this to them. It wasn't random. She could tell that they planned to pick them up specifically. For what she thought? No one knew of her money she had so who would want to hurt her. She knew Simone didn't really have any money so that was out the question also. Then her mind jumped to Trey. It could be someone trying to get back at Trey by hurting what he is closest to. Recently Trey has been real low key and hasn't been even doing the same things he was. He was focused on the music deal and she didn't know of anyone he had beef with. Besides, he was well respected around and couldn't imagine anyone stepping their boundaries in this way.

Just then it hit her. Simone committed the ultimate sin in the hood. She snitched on Roscoe and Gillie, Chantel thought to herself. 'Damn!' She knew that had to be it and was pissed off that she got caught up in it as well. Of course she didn't want anything to happen to either one of them but she cursed herself for allowing this to happen. She knew better than this.

In a few minutes she heard footsteps come close. It was more than one person. She felt Simone's body move from against hers. She was gone. She moved her legs around to feel for her but she was gone along with the footsteps. If Chantel ever feared anything it was this very moment. She was alone and had no idea what was going to happen next or where Simone was.

Chantel sat on the cold cement ground for hours. She didn't hear any more voices, sounds or footsteps for what felt like days. She nodded off into a light sleep ever so often but her nerves always jumped her out of it. She had no idea how much time passed or if it was morning by now. She decided it was now or never. She rolled onto her knees then stood up. She kicked in front of her to make sure she wasn't walking into anything. She slowly kicked and walked until she hit a wall. She turned around and used her palms to feel it and ran her hands across as she walked against it. It felt like bricks, she was pretty sure. She finally found a door.

Before she left the room she knew she had to get the bandanna off her eyes. She had to see where she was going. She placed her back against the wall and rubbed the back of her head up and down against the wall in an attempt to loosen up the bandanna. It worked; each time she rubbed the back of her head on the bricks it pulled it up and up. Finally it was off her head. Her eyes took a moment to adjust and she looked around. It was still night time, possibly early morning hours. She realized she was in what looked like an old abandoned factory building.

After quietly finding an exit, she ran until she could run anymore. Not sure where she was going, she just ran. She finally found a street with life, people, cars, and stores. She ran into the first store she could and begged them to call 911. Her heart raced as she waited for police to show up. She couldn't believe or understand that no one was left there to keep an eye on her. She wondered why but still paranoid they were following her.

Every second she kept looking behind her, around her, and down the street to make sure no one followed her. By sunrise the police came and checked out the old building. A detective approached Chantel to ask her some more questions about what happened.

"Chantel?" he asked as he sat down across from her in the coffee shop where she called 911.

"Yea?" she replied and looked up, sounding and looking exhausted.

"I hate to tell you this but your friend, Simone, she's gone," he sympathetically told her.

"Gone? She wasn't in there?"

"No, she was. We found her shot twice. She didn't make it. I'm so sorry," the detective responded. She froze; her heart skipped a beat, her mouth got dry. She couldn't speak; it was as if she lost her own life. This couldn't be real she thought.

Six months later

Chantel rolled over and sat up. She laid back down, not wanting to leave her warm bed. She twirled the wedding ring around her finger and smiled at the thought of being married to a rich, successful, handsome, honest man that she loved. Trey was her everything and she woke up every day thanking God that he sent him into her life. She reached over and ran her hands up his back.

After getting dressed she came back over to the bed and kissed him on the cheek, careful not to wake him. She had an early morning today and wanted to get up and out as soon as she could. As she fixed herself a light breakfast and sat in front of the TV. The news told their usual stories of murders, robberies, and traffic accidents in the area.

One story caught her full attention mentioning the name Roscoe. An instant pain shot through her chest at the reminder of losing her best friend. Roscoe was finally entering trial for the murder for hire he authorized on Simone. She thought about sitting in the court room during the trial and if she would be able to handle it. She had to though; for her friend. She also had to take the stand one day and relive detail by detail of when they were kidnapped.

Thinking back on that night she was so happy that Roscoe was only cheap enough to pay for the murder of one person and that was the sole reason her life was spared. It still devastated her that her friend was gone but she couldn't help but be grateful for her own life.

After watching the news story and gathering her thoughts she tried to refocus her mind. Her first stop of the day was to Chelsea Center for Recovery to visit her mother. She finally convinced her to get treatment for her problems and moved her out to NYC. With Trey's music doing so well, they were able to afford a great rehab program for her and so far it has been the best thing that she could have done. Closing in on thirty days sober, her mother was getting a second chance at life.

Even though things haven't always been great for Chantel, life seemed to be on her side lately. She thought about how her life was going the way that Simone's life should have went and Simone's life ended the way she expected her own too. Life is crazy that way she mused. Thankful for the desire to want more for her life, she completely turned it around.

The second stop of the day was to her doctor's office. She waddled through the door and took a seat in the waiting room. It was the day she found out if she was having a boy or a girl.

Acknowledgments

First I would like to thank my mom for always being a motivational force in my life!

Thanks to my friends for listening to me talk about this project for months and giving their help and opinions when need.

Also, I would like to thank Matt Merz for being so helpful and directing my trailer! Without your help I would have been lost! Thank you, Lionel Cook for shooting and editing. It came out great and you two did a perfect job of bring my vision to life! Thanks to all the actors and actresses who participated as well!

Thanks to my motivator and mentor, Stacey L. Moor. Thanks for passing your wisdom to me and helping me learn new things along the way.

Last, I would like to thank everyone who purchased this book! It has been a goal of mine for a while to write a book and with your support you have made it possible! This is just book number one, I promise to write more and get better with each one. Stay tuned!

- Jameelah

J.N.K Media
Jah423@gmail.com
www.TaleofGreed.com

CPSIA information can be obtained at www.ICGtesting.com
Printed in the USA
LVOW09s1411060215

426008LV00001B/13/P